AN ORDINARY VIOLENCE

A NOVEL

ADRIANA CHARTRAND

SPIDERLINE

Published in Canada and the USA in 2023 by House of Anansi Press Inc.
houseofanansi.com

House of Anansi Press is committed to protecting our natural environment.
This book is made of material from well-managed FSC®-certified forests,
recycled materials, and other controlled sources.

House of Anansi Press is a Global Certified Accessible™ (GCA by Benetech)
publisher. The ebook version of this book meets stringent accessibility
standards and is available to students and readers with print disabilities.

27 26 25 24 23 · 1 2 3 4 5

Library and Archives Canada Cataloguing in Publication
Title: An ordinary violence : a novel / Adriana Chartrand.
Names: Chartrand, Adriana, author.
Identifiers: Canadiana (print) 20230451942 | Canadiana (ebook) 20230451969
ISBN 9781487011888 (softcover) | ISBN 9781487011956 (EPUB)
Classification: LCC PS8605.H37 O73 2023 | DDC C813/.6—dc23

Book design: Greg Tabor
Cover image: *Black-Tailed Hare* (1841) painting in high resolution by John James
Audubon. Original from the Saint Louis Art Museum.

*House of Anansi Press is grateful for the privilege to work on and create from the
Traditional Territory of many Nations, including the Anishinabeg, the Wendat, and
the Haudenosaunee, as well as the Treaty Lands of the Mississaugas of the Credit.*

With the participation of the Government of Canada
Avec la participation du gouvernement du Canada | Canadä

*We acknowledge for their financial support of our publishing program the Canada
Council for the Arts, the Ontario Arts Council, and the Government of Canada.*

Printed and bound in Canada

MIX
Paper from
responsible sources
FSC® C103567

for my family and friends on the prairies

"Adriana Chartrand's *An Ordinary Violence* is a hallucinatory slow-burn chiller, sharply observed and heartfelt in its depiction of family ties that bind like strips of wet rawhide. Dawn returns to her hometown to find it is in the grip of something uncanny and malevolent. As she visits old friends and familiar places, she grapples with ghosts from the past and demons on the rise to save her struggling father, her wayward brother, and herself. With this fresh and fearsome look at the contemporary Indigenous experience, Chartrand emerges at the forefront of our newest literary voices."

—DAVID DEMCHUK, author of *The Bone Mother* and *RED X*

"*An Ordinary Violence* by Adriana Chartrand is a compelling read that rockets off the page. From the first chapter, I was hooked and gleefully followed Dawn as she moved around the spaces she used to call home to figure out her new reality. The writing is poetic, truthful, and you can tell that Adriana has written a story from her heart. This book will be sure to surprise its readers!"

—FRANCINE CUNNINGHAM, author of *God Isn't Here Today*

"*An Ordinary Violence* is surely a gripping and haunting novel, one that will hold you from the first word to the last, but what makes it so potent and memorable is the ways in which Adriana Chartrand tells this story with such grace and humility. There is horror, and then there is *horror—An Ordinary Violence* has both. This is an unforgettable novel."

—MORGAN TALTY, author of *Night of the Living Rez*

PROLOGUE

She's kneeling on cold ground.

Silent strobing of red and blue, lighting the frozen back lane.

A numb buzzing in her, through her. The low winter sky above.

Felt but unseen, shock waves lead up to and away from this moment. They crack and break and form a web, a pattern.

How can she still be there?

She wavers in and out, in and out, but of course, she's always still there.

She's coming undone. She fell, and is still falling.

The worst is yet to come.

Dirty, tire-tread snow, the red of the lights, and the red of those awful footprints.

Her brother's footprints—her brother's footprints walking away from her, outlined in the snow in blood.

Something has been set in motion, or was already moving, vast and churning, and the worst, the absolute worst, is coming.

CHAPTER ONE

The drive home takes Dawn three days. West, then north, down undulating highways, jockeying for space with the massive semis that burn past, rattling her small car and making her white-knuckle the wheel and swear under her breath. The landscape flattens by increments as she speeds along. Her calf cramps terribly, because she doesn't trust cruise control, because she doesn't drink enough water. She calls and books roadside motels for the night while she eats what passes for lunch at fluorescent-lit gas stations.

The highway at night is a strange, in-between space, a place that is no place. She's contained and suspended in her car, a pinprick of existence travelling outside of time.

3

The numbing sameness of the road allows her to make an uneasy peace with her thoughts that she needs right now. Still, her body is betraying her, cramping and hurting. Her stomach doing bigger flips the closer she gets.

There's a train at the crossing, so she throws the car in park and chews on her bottom lip. She's twenty minutes out from the city. The train rolls by slowly, its cars brown-brown-brown, then every colour, big looping graffiti covering every third or fourth car. They blur together, and she looks at the empty, open fields around her and realizes her lip is bleeding.

The train's last car rolls past. She drums her fingers on the steering wheel. The asphalt in the distance gleams with what looks like glistening water that constantly recedes as she approaches. She ignores her churning stomach and follows the vanishing water.

Everything looks the fucking same, Dawn thinks as she pulls onto the loose gravel driveway of her childhood home.

It's a bungalow with a grey slate roof. The A-frame roof hangs low, reaching for the grass on either side of the house, shrouding the windows and front door like a creature peering out from the underbrush. Dawn cuts the engine and sits behind the wheel, one leg jiggling restlessly up and down. The car is already heating up and beads of sweat roll from her hairline down her back, following a preordained route to the crack of her ass.

It's August, a month of long, oppressive days on the prairies. The sky is an imposing dome, clouds scudding low over the fields. Dawn shifts uncomfortably. August, with

4

everything beginning to teeter in its full ripeness toward decay, always turns her thoughts toward autumn. Then toward the coming winter.

In her father's driveway, she gets out of the car, dragging her overstuffed bag of belongings behind her. The bag is bulging and heavy, awkward to carry, but still holds a pretty pitiful collection. Everything she owns at twenty-nine years old, stuffed into a pink and black Reebok gym bag that scratches her arm with its rough Velcro strap. It's safe to say that her life in Toronto didn't turn out as planned. But she hadn't planned, had she? She doesn't want to think about that right now. She doesn't need to think, she just needs to do. Get through this rough patch, and then make a plan, a real one.

Don't think, she thinks, and heads for the front door.

The door opens onto the living room, small and dusty, the windows so dirty that what little light filters through is a mottled brown, like the mud-coloured river that cuts through the city. The rest of the room looks disused, covered in a layer of dust. Dawn takes in a darker patch of carpet with the exact dimensions of the floral couch that always sat there.

She stares for a few seconds at the bare spot, the room so familiar yet so strange. So sad and unlived in, it only confirms what she's been feeling: She shouldn't be here. She was free. She'd made it out. She emits a gulp or a moan, a desperate little hiccup, at the thought. As she gulps air, she catches a whiff of something foul.

Dawn strides into the kitchen, which opens off the living room, separated by a half-wall. The sink is piled high with dishes and mouldy pots sitting in brackish water. Bits of unidentifiable food cling to everything. Even with its door closed, the boxy white fridge, purchased when Dawn was twelve, is also contributing to the stench. A shiver of disgust passes over her as she pulls her T-shirt up over her nose. *How can Dad be living like this?*

When she'd last talked to her brother on the phone, trying to ignore the mechanical clicks in the background that meant they were being recorded, he'd given her an update on Martin.

"He's not doing too good, Dawn, you know," Cody had said softly down the phone. "He's drinking, and I guess he's pretty much moved into the basement? That's what Tyler said last time he checked up on him."

"Who the fuck is Tyler?" Dawn hadn't wanted to think about her dad holed up in the damp, semi-finished basement, quietly deteriorating.

"He's a friend, my buddy... He's been helping me out. Did you even hear what I said about Dad?"

That was nearly two months ago, before Dawn had known she'd be living with her father again. Before everything had gone to shit.

The stairs to the basement are off the kitchen, leading down to the dank rooms they'd all traditionally avoided. It was unfinished and cold, uninviting and creepy. They'd only ever used it for storage when Dawn was growing up. She keeps the T-shirt pulled up over her nose and mouth and heads for the stairs, disgust and—it's undeniable— anger building inside her.

She'd called that morning from the nearly empty parking lot, like a paved square of nothing dropped randomly from the sky, at the cheap motel in the Sioux where she'd stayed overnight, wind whipping her unwashed hair into her mouth no matter which way she turned. Her dad hadn't picked up. He knew she was coming back, and what day to expect her, but his memory was getting shoddier, and she worried that he would forget or change his mind about letting her stay. As much as it pains her to have to come home, she has nowhere else to go.

As she puts her foot on the top step, calling out, "Dad?" in an oddly tentative voice, she has an oily, queasy thought. A taunting, not unfamiliar thought. Her dad has worked for the same long-haul trucking company for thirty-six years, longer than Dawn's been alive. She's sure he's physically unhealthy after all these years, but he never goes to the doctor, and the idea that he may drop dead at any moment haunts her. Now, she sees an unwanted flash of a slumped figure, mouth open, on the floral couch, and her gut clenches. She descends a few steps, and then hears the sound of a crowd jeering, a referee counting down dramatically, an announcer narrating over it all—an old wrestling match from the nineties.

"Dad!" she calls a bit sharply and comes down the last steps. She stops on the quilted rug that covers the landing; the basement floor is raw concrete and Dawn is barefoot. She'd kicked off the flip-flops she's worn all summer long at the front door. She wishes she had them now. Another layer between her flesh and this house.

Martin is seated on the far end of the couch, which sits on a large, faded area rug, along with a dark wood TV cabinet, a TV (old as dirt and clunky as hell), and a standing lamp with a stained beige shade. The lamp throws a weak circle of light. There's a small window, high up and covered in grime that lets in the same filtered, murky light as the living room windows upstairs. The weak sunlight doesn't reach the frayed edge of the rug. The basement is shadowy, and a damp smell clings to the air: mildew and age and concrete.

Bleary-eyed behind thick glasses, her dad turns and sees her. "Oh!" he says, surprise turning to happiness. "Oh, Dawn. You're here."

Seeing her dad's eyes misting up behind the lenses of his glasses, Dawn's heart seizes in her chest, a quick, hard spasm of guilt. "Hey Dad," she says, forcing a smile. She shifts her weight awkwardly on the landing rug. Despite the heat of the day, the basement is distinctly chilly. "Uh, sorry, don't want to step on the floor...I'm not wearing my shoes..."

"Oh, honey, don't worry. Let me finish this match, okay, and I'll come upstairs. You had a good drive? Go put your stuff away and I'll meet you up there, order us some dinner. Haven't cooked much lately..."

His mild rambling betrays his drunkenness. The cloying stink of stale beer and whisky is in the air underneath the chill. Dawn flashes to the kitchen, the reeking sink and fridge. He'd never been like this, not until these few last years, but this was another level entirely. *What is he doing submerging himself down here?* she wonders, with no little disdain, but she immediately counters her own thought: *Hiding, like you*, and swats both thoughts away.

"That's okay, Dad. I'm meeting a friend for dinner tonight. I just wanted to say hi, let you know I'm here…"

Her dad lifts a thick glass tumbler of dark brown whisky from a small table, hidden in the shadows at the base of the standing lamp. He takes a sip and nods. "Okay, sweetie, okay." His eyes are dry now and glued to the screen. "I'll see you later, okay?"

"Okay," she replies, and ascends the stairs into the stink of the kitchen.

Suddenly, without knowing she's started to move, Dawn yanks open the cupboard under the sink and—thank god—finds garbage bags. Rips open the fridge, which is a post-apocalyptic landscape of rotting food, and throws everything into a garbage bag without looking. Tries to hold her breath. Gags, holds it again. She ties off the bag, opens the back door, and hurls it into the backyard. Runs hot water and empties the foul contents of every pot, pan, and bowl in the sink down the drain. Gags again. Throws all the cookware into another garbage bag, ties it off, and tosses it noisily into the yard. She storms into the bathroom and looks under the sink, where she hopes there will be an old bottle of Clorox spray. There is. She opens the fridge, coats the inside with bleach, and closes the door again. Sprays a foaming layer over the entire sink. Grabs her keys and her purse from beside her gym bag and is out the front door, gasping for air.

Her tight chest bursting, Dawn climbs into the silver Toyota and lays her forehead on the burning-hot steering wheel. She sits there and takes big gulps of steamy, stale air until her chest eases.

CHAPTER TWO

D awn cruises the streets slowly, driving in loops. She passes a squat beige stucco bungalow with an overgrown front lawn, colourful plastic toys abandoned in the grass. She imagines the kids who dropped the toys there when they were called inside to wash up and eat, sticky with late-summer sweat and wishing they could stay outside forever. Dawn remembers summer days like that. She passes a brown rancher overrun by garden decorations, a dizzying eyesore of pinwheels and gnomes and signs. A family of deer statues inches toward the sidewalk, trying to make their escape.

South Saint Jude is a neighbourhood cobbled together from bits of the history of this place, this land. The houses

11

are mostly older and smallish, with an in-between kind of feeling to them—not heritage homes and not new builds. Big trees, older than most of the houses, stretch over the front lawns. The public signs are in English and French. She passes the train tracks, the park, the old town hall that's now a post office. There's the low brick school and the lightly pitted soccer fields that the team from Crown Heights inevitably complains about each year. There's the small section of subsidized housing: row homes and four-unit apartment buildings shoved to the outskirts. Behind one of these buildings is the site of the semi-burnt-down monastery where nuns, most working as teachers in the community, used to live, and where kids now go to smoke joints and drink warm cans of Lucky, sitting in their parents' parked cars or on the crumbling stone walls, kicking their heels against the historic rocks. Everyone said the monastery was haunted, and it was easy to believe, especially at nighttime, headlights illuminating the piled stones and empty fields, a malicious feeling still emanating from the ruins.

The neighbourhood functions almost like a small town, attached to the southern outskirts of the city by a stretch of highway, the overpass acting as the unofficial barrier marking where the city proper ends. The city has expanded steadily over the last few decades, pushing its borders farther and farther out into the rolling fields and creeping closer to South Saint Jude. In a few more years, the area will no longer be on the outskirts but subsumed into the growing city, swallowed up. The new subdivisions all inevitably feature the same five models of two-storey, beige and grey stucco houses that rise from the churned mud. The visual monotony is broken by the occasional monstrosity of a McMansion: stone accents and stucco walls, turrets and bay windows thrown together haphazardly. On the edges of these subdivisions, sidewalks fall away into reedy ditches, reminding the residents that this was considered "the country" not too long ago. The newest one, across the highway and a field from the West End of South Saint Jude, is a warren of cul-de-sacs and identical townhouses, with one large, imposing square apartment block along its western edge, severe black-iron balconies jutting from the units. The building is a shock against the low-slung sky, rising several stories above the tallest homes. It is so incongruous, so out of place, that looking at it gives Dawn the dizzying feeling of inhabiting an alternate reality.

Dawn turns right after the long-suffering patch of grass and ancient play structure that passes for a park. The trees chatter in a rushed whisper, leaves stirring in the wind. A mass of deep grey clouds rears its head on the distant horizon. A day this hot and still is pleading for a storm to roll in.

One sticky summer day like this one during her wasteland high school years, Dawn went to get groceries to make tacos for dinner. Martin had come up with the idea, triumphant, then realized they needed taco shells, ground beef, lettuce, cheese. Dawn, bored, offered to go.

In line at the store, goosebumps on her bare legs and arms in the powerful A/C, Dawn lazily listened in on the conversation in front of her. The woman speaking was the volunteer guidance counsellor at the local middle school, which was attached to the high school, the two schools separated internally by a pair of locked double doors at the end of the main first-floor corridor. The middle school students could enter the high school only with a teacher chaperone when it was time to use the shared music room for band practice. The high school students were strictly barred from coming into the middle school, and one day, without explanation, a thick chain and padlock appeared looped several times around the doors, and they started having band practice in the math classroom.

The volunteer guidance counsellor was the brunette mother of three blond boy athletes, two of whom were known to be the school's most dedicated bullies. The father was a quiet, hulking man with the same white-blond hair as his sons and the ruddy cheeks of a drinker. He was standing silently behind his wife, who was chatting animatedly to the woman beside her, a teacher at the high school, who nodded along with pursed lips.

"The guy's bad news, if you ask me."

"Didn't the mother die a few years ago?"

"She did, yeah. An Indian, right? The mother?"

Dawn's heart froze.

"Yeah, that weird Aboriginal woman," the father said in his slow voice.

And then one of the women—their voices sounded the same to Dawn—said with a sigh, like it pained her that she couldn't figure it out, "I don't know why they can't just stick with their own."

Dawn ran out of the store, her chest aching, her face burning so hot she thought it might ignite. As she hustled by, her elbow caught one of the women in the ribs. Her startled cry followed Dawn out the automatic sliding doors.

When she got home, sweating, she walked straight to her room, Martin's "Did you get the groceries?" fading behind her.

An hour later, her father knocked on her door, pizza box in hand like a peace offering, even though he'd done nothing wrong. Dawn felt a specific and familiar pang of guilt, its contours and weight so well known to her heart. She gave in and followed him to the kitchen, where he talked about his rec league hockey team while Dawn nodded along. He didn't ask again about the groceries, and she didn't volunteer anything.

Cody wasn't there, and neither of them mentioned that, either.

Being back where she grew up is making her head spin. As she cruises the too-familiar streets, Dawn realizes suddenly that she's driven on autopilot to Crystal's house. Inseparable from ages two to twelve, Dawn and Crystal grew up in each other's bedrooms and backyards. They built forts in the sparse woods along the western edge of their neighbourhood, accidentally fell into the slow, shallow creek, the water up to their hips, and wrapped themselves in oil-stained blankets from Crystal's dad's shed until they'd avoided their parents long enough to dry off. They passed hours lying on each other's beds or the identical ugly beige carpets on their bedroom floors, writing in the pink-covered journals Crystal's mom bought them, painting each other's toes with red nail polish (that Dawn self-consciously hid from her brother and father when she got home), talking about which classmates they liked or disliked that week. That closeness had fallen away slowly, and then quickly, as they entered the uncharted territory of high school, each looking for how and where to slot themselves into the pre-established social fabric.

It is the natural state of all things to ebb and flow, Dawn reminds herself. This is a favoured mantra from her boss in Toronto, meant to inspire calm and acceptance in the face of adversity. Dawn repeats it to herself in the hope that one day soon it will inspire this in her. But for now, she fights to keep the image of a rushing river, white foam crashing against hard rock, out of her mind.

As she slowly approaches the house, she sees a woman standing on the small porch, beckoning fervently. Dawn stares for a moment, even though she recognizes the woman right away. It's Elena Cleary, Crystal's mom. Mrs. Cleary is smiling and waving, her arm jiggling in time.

Get it together, Dawn tells herself. She pulls the car over to the curb and tries to park as naturally as possible, as though she meant to drop by. *Why was she just standing on her front porch?* Dawn wonders. She forces herself to get out of the car, smiling and waving at Mrs. Cleary.

"Uh, hey!" she calls out, and stands awkwardly, not moving toward the house.

"Dawn, my dear! How lovely that you'd pull up just

now—we're just about to have supper! Crystal and the kids are here! Please come eat with us!"

Mrs. Cleary's unrestrained enthusiasm is jarring, but Dawn has no way to explain her sudden presence outside her home, so she walks toward the house, cursing herself internally for her stupid, languid, nostalgic cruise. She could have stayed hidden inside her dad's house for as long as she needed and not even registered as a blip on the neighbourhood's radar.

Mrs. Cleary beams as Dawn climbs the steps of the tiny porch, an addition in blond wood that doesn't match the rest of the house, built by Mr. Cleary the summer of grade five. She remembers how the smell of sawdust drifted over her and Crystal as they tanned and sipped powdered iced tea in the backyard where the lumber was kept. She has a flashback to walking down a craterous aisle at Costco, where her own family did not have a membership, Crystal throwing a gigantic plastic tub of iced tea mix into the cart Dawn pushed along.

"You're back in town, Dawn! Just lovely. My, it's been years since we've seen you around here." Mrs. Cleary rests a big, callused hand on Dawn's shoulder and guides her toward the open front door. "How long are you staying?"

"I, uh, I'm not sure actually ... I'm staying with my dad for a bit, helping out around the house ..." Dawn mutters evasively.

"Well, isn't that lovely. We hope you'll stay a while, of course."

They step into the neat front hall decorated with cream

and gold patterned wallpaper—big, bold, but slightly muted swirls of gold that remind Dawn of a corporate office's waiting room.

Mrs. Cleary bustles past Dawn toward the back door and calls over her shoulder, "Just leave your shoes on, dear. We're all out in the backyard!"

Dawn straggles through the living room and kitchen. No way to put the brakes on now. The walls of the kitchen are still covered in the decorative sayings that have hung there for as long as she can remember. *I'd Rather Be in Bed* is in black cursive on a blue background, above a cartoon woman with platinum hair cooking in a chaotic-looking kitchen, and *I Saved the Wine—It Was Trapped in the Bottle!* is in painstaking needlepoint, done by Mrs. Cleary, complete with an embroidered glass of red wine. The commandment *Be Happy!* in giant curling letters is burned rustically into a striped wooden paddle that hangs above the sink.

Dawn steps through the back door into a blinding shaft of sunlight, throwing up her hand to cover her eyes. She sees an odd silhouette of people gathered in the yard, forming a circle, facing inwards. She blinks from behind the visor of her hand and the vision is gone.

People are sitting in lawn chairs with beers in the cupholders, plates of burgers and potato salad balanced awkwardly on their knees, or smoking and laughing over by the fence. A fold-out table holds the food and drinks—beer, wine coolers in cans, and several two-litres of pop, going flat in the heat. A few kids are running and screaming over by the fence, playing a game that seems to involve

AN ORDINARY VIOLENCE

a lot of shoving. A small child falls to the ground and emits a high-pitched, searing wail. Dawn looks around but none of the adults moves to comfort or claim the child, who, after a moment, crumples like all their energy has been sapped and lies there quietly, picking at the grass. Dawn's weariness after the long drive is sinking deep into her bones, but she summons a smile for the woman striding toward her, arms thrown wide with incredulity.

"Dawn! What the hell are you doing here? I mean … god! It's been years!"

With a jolt, Dawn realizes the woman is Crystal, years older and with dyed hair, a startlingly complex layered arrangement of blond and reddish highlights and lowlights. Crystal's thin frame is toned and lithe—and tanned. Dawn doesn't remember her ever being so tan. She's wearing pilled black yoga pants, a stretchy work-out tank top, and plastic flip-flops. Her finger- and toenails are painted turquoise, and she has a nose piercing, a big diamond stud that juts out jarringly from her narrow face. She still has thin lips and high cheekbones, but her eyes have dark circles so deep they look like bruises. Dawn tells herself to stop concentrating on people's flaws.

Before Dawn has a chance to speak, Crystal is hugging her, pulling Dawn firmly into her toned sternum and perky (fake?) breasts. She smells of that late-summer mixture of sweat and perfume, some kind of floral-scented shampoo. Dawn hugs her back, then pulls away, probably too quickly.

"Crystal! I…It's so nice to see you, to see your mom,

again. I'm just … here helping my dad out for a bit." Dawn feels like her equilibrium has been thrown off ever since she pulled into her dad's driveway, like she's walking on shaky ground.

"Dawn, wow! Come on, come sit by me. You've got to meet my husband, Jake."

Crystal leads Dawn toward the concrete patio, a flat square crushing the grass, with a clunky all-weather table in the middle surrounded by heavy-looking chairs. A retractable awning is cranked out on its plastic arm to provide shade from the relentless sun. *Wasn't there a storm coming?* Dawn wonders. The sky is hazy with heat but clear. There's a faint charge in the air like before a thunderstorm, like electricity building.

Jake is sprawled casually in a white plastic lawn chair that's too small for his big frame. He's a tall, broad man, with muscles that are just starting to go soft now that he's a husband, a father—he's earned the cushy extra layer pushing his midsection over his brown leather belt. His close-cropped dusty-blond hair is covered by a Bruins hat. There's a kind of languid grace, gained from a lifetime of confidently occupying a body, in the way he stretches out from the chair, leaning backwards, elbows propped on the armrests, long legs in front and crossed at the ankles. He looks at Dawn and his wife approaching, a glimmer in his eyes behind the hooded lids under the hat.

He raises his beer in greeting. "Hi, honey. And who's this?"

Jake's voice is long and low, hard consonants and twanging vowels, a deep prairie-boy rhythm. He's probably from one of the farms that skirt the area. If you keep driving south along the highway that leads into South Saint Jude and don't branch off into the residential streets, you will hit the open fields. Gravel roads mark a sloppy grid across the muddy fields, all rushing to rejoin the main artery—the highway that will take you all the way down to Texas if you stay on it long enough, farms dotting the landscape on either side.

Jake looks like a hockey player—sloping shoulders and well-muscled thighs and at least three missing teeth. Well past his glory days, even though he's probably only in his mid- to late thirties. Boys who grew into men like him are ubiquitous here. Throw a rock anywhere and hit one. Despite high-school-era pro-athlete dreams, they tend to end up in the family business: construction and development in the North, admin for the oil rigs over in Alberta. They keep their past dreams alive by over-zealously coaching their kids' hockey teams, taking swings at other parents in the community centre bleachers, screaming at the twelve-year-olds on the ice.

Dawn knows this kind of man. She smiles at Jake, uncomfortable. Jake's older than her brother, but boys like him weren't shy about starting fights with Cody after school, like they were defending the neighbourhood's honour.

"I'm Dawn. Old friend of Crystal's." She makes herself extend her hand to him. "I grew up here—just around the corner, actually. Just back here for a bit, helping my dad."

Her throat is sore. She doesn't know why she says all that. It feels like a confession, like it was forced out of her.

Jake sits up straight in his chair and smiles powerfully at her, a big beam of a smile she's sure he's employed many times, for many different reasons.

"Hi, Dawn, nice to meet you." He shakes her hand. "You grew up here, eh? Funny we've never met before.'

Dawn shrugs. She spent the years after Violet's death straying alone. Martin provided no real companionship; he was a planet orbiting in a different galaxy from his children.

Jake leans back in his chair again, takes a sip of his beer. Crystal is smiling and nodding encouragingly, but Dawn isn't sure what she's encouraging. Dawn feels tired and disoriented, dizzy. Like she can't quite get her feet steady underneath her long enough to look around and figure out where she is. The feeling that she should not be here, that being here is not right, hits her forcefully. She hopes she is still smiling. The sun is dipping across the sky, trailing its heat and baking them underneath it. Jake is staring at her from beneath his hat. Dawn starts to sweat. She should leave.

Crystal motions toward a chair in the shade of the colossal, cranked-out awning. "Sit down, Dawn. I'll grab you a beer. Do you want something to eat?"

Dawn wants to say no, because accepting food feels like accepting they're friends again or something, but she's hungry.

"I'll have some macaroni salad, if you don't mind," she says, and Crystal is off across the yard, flip-flops slapping her pedicured heels.

Jake taps the bottom of his beer bottle against his knee in

an irritating rhythm, and Dawn despairs at being left alone with him. She's out of practice at striking up conversations with the kind of man she grew up around. In Toronto, Frances would prepare their dinners in such a neat and organized fashion; he'd fold his clothes perfectly after doing the laundry. Dawn is willing to bet that Crystal does all of Jake's laundry.

"What are you helping your dad with?" Jake asks, and Dawn is startled to realize she doesn't have a response.

"Just … you know … life," she says vaguely and looks away, looks directly at the sun, hoping this will disguise her flaming face.

He nods like this is an acceptable answer and takes a sip of beer. "We could all use some help with that once in a while," he affirms and winks at her.

She bristles. It's not a lewd wink—that's not the problem. It's the familiarity, like they share an inside joke about the trials and tribulations of life that Dawn is certain they do not, cannot, share.

She wills her anger away, wills it away. Dawn is trying really hard to let go of her anger in general, to release herself from its toxic grip. She has to feel it but not give in to it. She has to be angry and not be angry. At least she's always known how to be two things at once.

Just be normal, she tells herself. "How long have you and Crystal been married?" she volleys at Jake to break her silence. She knows how long they've been married because it's been on Crystal's Facebook profile since February 14, 2010. Dawn has also perused several photo albums more than once, marvelling at the spectacle of their wedding in a voyeuristic and frankly rude way that she doesn't feel great about—but, still, she does it.

One of the albums is titled *Our Song*—a dump of twenty-seven photos of Crystal and Jake during their first dance, all very similar, most from the same angle, many blurry. They danced to "I Don't Want to Miss a Thing" by Aerosmith, a song that makes Dawn think of fiery comets plunging through the earth's atmosphere and heading straight for her.

There's another album titled *Best Night of My Life* <3 that is a collection of random shots from the ceremony, reception, and after-party. In the pictures from the after-party at her mom's place, Crystal is visibly wasted but still grinning happily. In one, she's kneeling in her wedding dress on the kitchen floor, Jake tipping red wine from a cardboard box with a plastic spout into her open mouth. She's captioned it with the monkey-hiding-its-face emoji and the crying-laughing emoji.

"Winter 2010," Jake declares with a puff of pride, like he's recalling a particularly good hunting season.

"That's nice," Dawn says and looks for Crystal. She's over at the food table, which isn't shaded from the sun (*is the food spoiled?*), chatting with an older woman. Dawn squints and definitely sees the creamy macaroni salad looking suspect in the heat.

Just as Dawn decides it's time to say goodbye to Jake, to this whole little shindig, two little boys come rocketing over and throw themselves at Jake's lap, pointy elbows and blond hair flying as they squeal with open delight. Jake pats them both on the back of the head, and they yell something unintelligible, then take off running again, across the yard.

"My sons," Jake says, unnecessarily.

"They're so sweet," Dawn offers. "How old are they? What are their names?"

"They're four. Pride of my life. Joy of my life. Tanner and Tyson."

"What a good age," she says, having no idea what people even mean when they say that. Those kids could be little monsters for all she knows.

"Excellent age. Hard to believe, though. Time flies, time flies."

Like most men from around here, Jake is a man of few words. Somewhere around the last few years of adolescence, they fall silent—with each other, with their women. Silence can mean anything. The men don't talk and the women guess and guess, and try to predict what they might want, preferably before they even know themselves, so they'll have time to get it ready. Nervous wives finish the last of their work for the day and head home, make supper. Wait and see.

Crystal is back, beer and a paper plate heaped with macaroni and potato salad in hand. She gives them both to Dawn, who thanks her and puts the beer into the chair's cupholder, balances the plate on her knees. Disgust rises in her throat at the sight of the lump of—surely—spoiled potatoes, next to the congealed macaroni.

Crystal leans down to kiss Jake on the head. She looks across the yard at her sons, her hand over her eyes to block the sun. "What the hell are they doing over there?" she asks no one in particular. There's a new, harsh edge to her words. "They shouldn't be doing that," she declares and marches off to collect her sons, who Dawn suddenly feels sorry for.

Alone with Jake again, Dawn cannot muster the energy for another attempt at conversation. She puts the still-full plate on the ground near her chair and picks up the beer.

"Great to meet you, Jake. Please tell Crystal thanks for the, uh, hospitality. We should hang out again soon! I'm just really tired... from my drive."

She's already backing away as she talks, and Jake looks at her with his lip curled in a bemused expression. He looks pointedly at the beer she's holding.

"Roadie." She raises it in a salute, then turns and walks quickly toward the gate. She's nearly there when she feels a hand tug on her shoulder. She turns to see Crystal, who is now gripping her arm tightly; for a fraction of a second Crystal's face appears as a blank, white skull, a living hand touching her and the bareness of death looking her in the eyes. Dawn steps backwards and nearly gasps before she recovers. Crystal looks completely normal. A trick of the light.

"Going already?" Crystal asks, sounding genuinely disappointed.

Dawn offers up an apologetic look. "It was great to see you, but I can't stay!" she says while backing away. Crystal looks somewhat perplexed.

"Okay, well, bye!" Dawn says too cheerfully, turns and slips out the gate, and half-jogs to her car.

She drives away quickly, not caring where she's headed, just needing to leave. She tells herself she's exhausted, and that's why her mind is playing tricks on her, that's why she's so desperate to get away, that's why she has a feeling of dread, building to a crescendo.

She turns on the radio and it's static, a garbled song breaking through. Just as a woman's voice comes through clearly, she slaps at the button, turning it off.

She drives in silence, her knuckles white on the wheel.

CHAPTER THREE

D awn drives the straight shot of highway downtown. The highway runs through the city, cutting it almost evenly in half and serving as the main conduit between the South and North Ends. She's done the boring drive from her place in the South End to downtown many times, often with no other purpose than to be out of the house and alone.

In the last two decades the downtown area has undergone a series of "revitalization" efforts, none ever quite finding a lasting foothold. Of course, what the city meant by revitalization was gentrification, but the scrappy spirit of downtown wasn't broken. Residents asked for roads to be repaved, buildings repaired, outdoor lights installed, and nice public spaces built. The city responded with the latest project: an almost comically out-of-place "entertainment complex" behind the woefully underfunded public library.

The complex is composed of an upscale Italian restaurant decorated with fake lemon tree branches, as though the pieces of plastic will transport diners from the narrow urban streets to a stunning Capri coastline; a takeout Thai place; a rec room (rows of overpriced arcade games); and a few clothing boutiques. It looks like it's been plunked down from above, and its brick courtyard (sold in the developer's plans as a "public park-like space") is empty, save for an elderly man walking in a looping circle and pointing vehemently at the ground. The new benches are bisected by steel handles to prevent anyone from sleeping on them for the night.

Dawn takes a wrong turn in the confusing maze of one-way streets and ends up momentarily lost. The streets are an illogical mix of residences and businesses, a combination of old-school family-owned diners and tailors and pawnshops, and the types of stores that won't fly in the city's conservative suburbs—a head shop, a sex shop, and a fortune teller working out of her basement, advertised with a small neon sign flashing pink and green tarot cards, a purple crystal ball. Once Dawn spots Ezmerelda's, she realizes she needs to go right at the next intersection.

The dingy sign for Al's Eats & Beverages over the front door is faded and chipped, but Dawn is very glad to see it. It's still the same sign from when she was a teenager and would sit in the back of the lounge with Cody and some of his friends, sneaking booze into their pop and ordering chicken fingers and fries to share. She pushes open the front door and the same smell from back then hits her: cabbage and the heat cranked too high and whisky. She makes her way to a cracked vinyl booth half-covered with duct tape and sits under a thick, antique-looking mirror that she worries vaguely will fall and break her skull open. She's glad the place hasn't changed, but a few upgrades wouldn't be misplaced, she thinks, shifting to avoid the sharp edges of one of the cracks in her seat.

The air is that particular kind of musty that only comes from many years of smoking indoors, the nicotine seeping into the carpet and furniture, into every inch of fabric and fixture. The owner (and only bartender/server) is an eighty-year-old Ukrainian man who evidently doesn't give a shit about smoking laws, with wrinkles so deep his eyes have vanished into the folds of his face. Dawn's never bothered to ask if this man is Al.

She orders a double whisky and ginger ale, which is served in a dirty tumbler. She gulps it down. For a moment, her head swims, and then a pleasant warmth spreads through her, replacing the clench of nausea in her gut and soothing her jangling nerves.

She raises two fingers to request another double. *What a sad circle this is*, she thinks ruefully. The backs of her thighs below her sweat shorts stick to the cheap booth, vinyl fusing with flesh in the cramped heat of the bar. Her eyes sting. Her body feels ungainly, uncontrolled, spreading out and sticking to things. She's trapped by the heat, bound by it to be constantly reminded of her fleshly being.

The ice is mostly melted in the glass by the time the drink is in front of her. The old man brings it over and pushes it across the tabletop on a thick cardboard coaster advertising beer. She nods at him and grabs the drink. It goes down fast.

She'd never, not ever, considered that she might one day be back here, not just at Al's but here, in this city, this place. The possibility had not existed for her when she'd left. The possibility of return. She doesn't know how she's supposed to feel. Is she starting fresh or repeating the past? She can't shake the idea that she's back-pedalled through the years of her life, rewound the tape. Or is it that she's come all the way back around to the beginning?

A circle or a straight line, the outcome is the same.

The whisky, as always, whispers in her ear of the past, and she gives in and plunges backwards.

Dawn was standing in the front yard in the springtime, her mother beside her. Violet's long hair was tied back in a low ponytail underneath her ball cap—she often wore an old Dodgers hat, though Dawn is certain she knew nothing about the Dodgers. The big maple tree in the front yard was spreading its crown wide over their heads, its mottled grey-brown branches sprouting bright green buds and the first new leaves. The sun was regaining its strength, but the air still carried a chill, so Dawn was wearing her favourite jacket, a neon pink and green windbreaker that crackled pleasingly when she moved.

She can no longer remember why she and her mother were outside that day, but they were standing side by side in the front yard, looking down at a dead baby bird under the maple tree, its small eyes filmed over with white, like smoky pearls. Violet was not often physically affectionate, so neither is Dawn; she's not comfortable and easy with hugs, with casual arm touches. Still, on this day, Violet placed her hand on top of Dawn's head, her palm sending warmth deep inside her. And Dawn leaned against her mother's angular side for a moment before breaking away.

Violet, Martin, Cody, and Dawn were the totality of their family unit. Martin's parents died when Dawn was one year old. There are two photographs of them, serious-looking and pale, his mother's hair pressed into flat old-fashioned ringlets and her lips drawn down, his father's chest pushed out and his eyes hard. They have no photos of Violet's family, and she never spoke of them after they vanished from their lives when Dawn and Cody were young. Dawn imagines a row of shadowy, blanked-out silhouettes, forever unknown.

A month after Dawn and Violet found the bird, their unit collapsed. The parents told the kids that Violet was dying, claimed by a cancer that wasn't found by the doctors until it was too late for treatment. Violet was sitting on the grey couch in the living room, gaze directed out the window to the empty street. Martin was standing awkwardly beside her, and when he put a heavy hand on Violet's thin shoulder, she looked up at him with surprise, as though she'd forgotten he was there. She told Martin she'd rather die than die in a hospice. He laughed through his red, red eyes and hugged his thin, sick wife and promised she'd be as comfortable as possible in their bedroom. Then Violet opened her arms to Dawn and Cody, who were standing numbly in front of their parents, absorbing the information. Dawn folded eagerly into her mother's arms, but Cody ran out the front door, slamming it shut. They watched him pace the front yard in angry, jerky movements before he came back inside and headed straight for his room.

The next day, Violet was bedridden and could only get up with help from Martin to use the bathroom and bathe. Dawn was too young to understand what was meant to ease her mother's suffering and what was part of the disease; the morphine syringes and pills scattered on the bedside table for two weeks became twisted up with Violet's pain, and Dawn believed in some part of the back of her mind, even for a long time after knowing it wasn't true, that it was the injections and medications that Martin gave Violet that made her sick. Dawn wanted to ask Violet to stop, to stay, but she never had the words to ask her mother these kinds of things.

As Violet dwindled, the family removed themselves from time. Dawn and Cody watched TV in the living room, the volume turned up. Cody made them grilled cheese sandwiches for dinner, and Martin moved the armchair into the bedroom and sat beside Violet day and night. Dawn crept quietly into the bedroom, stuffy and septic-smelling, to stand beside her sleeping mother for a few minutes. She reached out and touched her black hair, stuck to her head with sweat and straggly on the white pillowcase but still thick and long.

One night shortly before Violet died, Dawn overheard Martin on the phone with Violet's doctor, who called at the end of each day. Dawn crouched out of sight behind the living room wall to listen.

"She's ready to go now," Martin said.

Her mother—ready to go from the earth. From her. Dawn's small heart clenched. Martin's words landed so deeply they remained with her for the rest of her life.

On the day Violet died, in the moments after, Dawn stood frozen in the living room, unable to move, and Cody walked out the back door and into the backyard, now overgrown with grass and weeds, and stood there helplessly, pointlessly, eyes closed against it all. Cody stood alone in the backyard with the wind whipping against his neck and cheeks, whipping away his tears. Where it passed the last houses before the open fields, the wind howled, calling out across the long, lonely plains.

Dawn didn't see Violet again for seven years after she died. Then Violet came to her one day, in the sunshine, as Dawn was cutting through the park on her way home from school. That first time, her mother spoke through a boy playing soccer in the patchy field. He was kicking his ball against the side of a concrete maintenance hut, but the ball bounced off in all directions half the time rather than coming back to him. So Dawn thought he was chasing the ball when he came up to her. She turned to face him just as he reached her, and he stretched out his small hand to touch the sleeve of her light fall jacket, tentatively, lightly. Still, his fingertips imparted an electrical thrill, and the little boy looked up at her with blank eyes, and it was Violet's voice that said: *"Don't."* And then the boy shook his head and ran back toward his ball.

The sun cut through a film of clouds and Dawn stood still, stunned, in its light, feeling herself to be a hollow thing, pierced by its rays.

Now, Dawn finishes her drink and presses the heels of her hands into her eyelids until she sees deep purple spots, then releases them quickly, enjoying the sensation of being temporarily unable to see. She drums her fingertips on the table, knowing it's time to go home but resisting. She can't really delay much longer unless she plans on staying here and getting piss drunk, which she knows is a piss-poor idea. She waits another ten minutes anyway.

Finally, she gets up to pay her tab, pushes a five-dollar tip across the sticky bar top, and leaves. She avoids driving past the Cleary residence on the way home to her dad's place. The first thing she notices after she parks is that the light is on in the front window. The night air is still warm, and Dawn walks slowly up the drive. Her dad opens the front door before she gets there, swinging it wide, trying to tell her something. The smell of stale booze coming off him mingles with Dawn's fresh whisky mouth and she is suddenly very, very tired.

"Dad, what? I can't understand you." Dawn moves toward her father, finally catching what he's saying as she moves past him into the house.

"Your brother, Dawn! Cody's coming home!"

They're sitting at the kitchen table now.

"He's getting out early for good behaviour. Reduced sentence? I think that's what he called it." Martin lifts his beer in a happy toast and takes a long, satisfied pull. "Wow!" he marvels, almost to himself.

Dawn forces a smile, remembers her last conversation with Cody on the phone.

"Dad, who's Tyler?" she asks.

Martin blinks. "Who, honey?"

"Tyler? Cody mentioned him...on the phone before. Said he'd been by here."

Martin crinkles a smile at his daughter. "Been by here? None of Cody's pals come by here anymore."

There's an unpleasant smell in the kitchen: bitter, like smoke.

Her brother's release date is set for less than a month away. It feels like that moment, that split second, when the back wheels of your car hit black ice and you start to skid. You start to lose control, and you know it's happening. It feels just like that—like an inevitable crash.

A sharp sound startles Dawn and she raises her head from her hands, bleary-eyed. A bird lies on the thin sill outside the front window, perfectly still. A tiny, starred crack in the glass. Dawn stares at the bird, a sick dread rising from below her ribs.

CHAPTER FOUR

TORONTO

Dawn arrived in Toronto late at night and used a key left in a little envelope in the spider-webbed mailbox to let herself in. She then collapsed, exhausted, in her new basement room, which came furnished with a queen-sized bed that sat on a lightly stained box spring and a large, solid-looking pine dresser. The bed was too hard, but she didn't care; she fell into a deep, dreamless sleep.

She met her roommates slowly over the course of the next day as they woke up or came home from school or work. They all passed through the big, somewhat grungy shared living room on the main floor, where Dawn sat watching TV on her laptop with headphones, and said friendly-seeming hellos before they left to shower downstairs, or cook in the spacious but shabby kitchen attached to the living room, or whatever activity they were doing in the privacy of their rooms. Having roommates was a new experience for Dawn, and she found herself imagining what each of them was doing in their rooms but stopped, feeling perverted, when her thoughts inevitably turned to masturbation.

That first evening, they all gathered on the semi-rotted back porch, passed around a joint, and officially welcomed Dawn to the fold. It was a warm summer night. The unkempt backyard stretched into blackness beyond the faint light cast by a single bulb over the back door; wild bushes and trees and overgrown weeds loomed along the fence-line, spectral in the dusk. Dawn had found this place through an online ad and had spoken to her future room-mates over Skype. They'd asked her to move in and she'd packed her things and drove to Toronto the next day. Now here she was, pretending to enjoy the bush weed they were smoking, but still—having a pleasant time hanging out with her new roommates. It was a promising start.

Casey was a smart and funny Korean Canadian busi-ness student on scholarship at U of T who still managed to party more than Dawn thought humanly possible. She was from a small town a few hours' south and went back to visit her mother and stepdad only at Christmas. Casey's long, pale fingers brushed Dawn's as she passed her the joint again, and that little intimate moment felt good. Dawn told herself she was happy. She smoked the bad weed, and then passed the joint along to Gracie.

Gracie, with her weird teen-girl name, was petite and elfin. Her dark brown hair somehow offset her cutesy name and small stature, made her seem bold and serious—though the illusion of seriousness broke as soon as she smiled or laughed, which she did often. She was what she called "a creative." She painted sometimes and sculpted sometimes, out of "non-traditional" materials, and danced sometimes and was, in general, constantly moving and making (and talking about it as she went). Part of Dawn wanted to hate her, immediately and viscerally, but she knew that this was really a simmering envy and she pushed it down. She envied Gracie's seeming freeness, her assured movements, her confidence when she showed them the latest thing she'd made. That night, she sat perched on a rough-looking wooden bench, her legs drawn up to her chest, folding herself up so delicately, like a perfect pixie. She unfolded herself, reached for the magnum of cheap white wine, and poured some more into Dawn's mason jar.

The third roommate, Frances, was a gentle history major working steadily toward his PhD. Quiet and polite, he smiled shyly at Dawn while they talked in the dying light of the summer night but joined them all in uncontrollable laughter when one side of Casey's chair crunched through a rotten board, tilting her onto the deck like a bucking bronco. The house was old and not very well taken care of, but it was cheap in an expensive city. The landlords were a young couple with a small, doe-eyed child who never once spoke to Dawn the entire time she lived below them.

"Say hi!" the parents would implore, urging the kid out from behind their legs where he'd be cowering. He staunchly refused.

The house was near the end of a long residential street, at the far west end of a neighbourhood some people, mainly university friends of Frances's, were afraid to come to. There were two halfway houses on their street. The men who stayed there would sit on the front porch, and often the lawn, and smoke ceaselessly. Their arms and hands would move from lap to lip like robots, like the mechanical arms of slot machines. With their hoods pulled up, they smoked and smoked, and Dawn hoped their reintegration into society was going well but also avoided eye contact when she walked past, pretended not to hear the occasional catcall that followed in her wake.

Being in the city felt like an incredible expansion. Her mind was reaching up and up here, instead of creeping out and out, like it did at home. Her mind followed the city's skyscrapers and signature tower, reached for the stars, and told her there were possibilities. There was a future here. The city had a siren call, and she was following it. What did the siren call promise her? What did it sound like, in her ear? Anything. Anything other than what was.

DAWN SOON GOT a job at a nearby dive bar. She'd never bartended before, but the owner, who was friendly and sweaty and knew Gracie, or knew someone who Gracie knew, didn't seem to mind. Dale had her demonstrate opening a bottle of beer and a bottle of wine, then gave her a thumbs-up. She smiled but told herself to hide how thrilled she was.

The bar was small, as most bars in the city turned out to be. On nights out with her roommates, Dawn was dismayed to discover that many bars were glorified hallways—tight, cramped, overheated spaces with music blasting loud enough to discourage much thinking.

The bar Dawn worked at was called Pete's, and it was a double-wide hallway with a bar along one wall, plus a small front room and a small back room (three tables in each small room)—palatial by Toronto standards. She'd replaced the previous bartender, a girl named Becca who'd moved back to Ohio, and worked five nights a week, including Fridays and Saturdays. One night, a regular mentioned how sorry she was about Becca, the bartender, and Dawn asked what she meant.

"Oh, well, she died, you know. The girl who used to work here? Guess you didn't know her. Her boyfriend killed her when she said she was leaving him. It was on the news for a bit."

When Dawn asked Dale about it, anger bubbled up in her and spilled over, unexpectedly. "She didn't move back to Ohio, Dale! She died! She was murdered!"

Dale glanced over at her, then back at the TV in the corner, continued to channel surf. "Oh damn," he said. "For some reason, I thought she moved back to Ohio. Must have been someone else." He settled on a show about hunting for monstrous fish in rivers. Dawn couldn't think of anything else to say.

The regulars were a mixture of somewhat grizzled, older hipsters, students, and just regular young people, all of whom disappeared into the bathroom in twos and threes to share tiny baggies of heavily cut coke. Dawn knew that Dale partook constantly throughout their shifts, but he was the kind of sad that's trapped inside of itself, not the kind that gets aimed out at other people as anger. He didn't get too intense or weepy, just sweat-soggy, and he'd usually just watch TV or talk on the phone in the back room, so it worked out fine.

In spite of its numerous flaws, Dawn loved the little bar. While it was mostly quiet on weeknights, when she didn't mind hanging out behind the bar, reading a book, and occasionally serving lone customers and small groups, it was always loud and bustling on weekends—so hot and busy that all Dawn could think about, by necessity, was the task at hand: grabbing a glass, getting ice, pouring a drink. She loved losing herself in the repetitive physical movements because it allowed her a reprieve from her own mind, always racing, racing. Her thoughts ground to a halt and her mind blanked out as she focused on the work, and she was grateful, above all else, for this escape.

It was a good gig, and her roommates often dropped by on the weekends to start or end their night out with free shots from Dawn. Well, technically, from Dale, who always waved vaguely in their direction in response to their shouted greetings, even though Dawn knew he didn't ever recognize them and had no idea who they were, other than Gracie.

Then Frances started to come by almost every night she worked, to sit at the end of the bar doing homework or research, or whatever he was doing, something related to his PhD thesis. He drank his beer slowly and smiled shyly up at her whenever she got within three feet of him. When she wasn't busy, she leaned her elbows on the counter and they talked easily, flirting over the scarred wooden bar top. He talked about his family and life back in Ottawa, where he'd grown up, and his thesis, and she tried to listen, to be fully engaged, even when he went off on tangents and they both lost the thread of what he was saying. She told simple lies about her life back home, about her friends and her family and the kinds of things she did in her free time. She wanted to keep things light and easy.

She liked Frances. She did. And that was good because suddenly (it seemed sudden—it seemed like there was no before or after, like she couldn't pinpoint when it started) they were dating.

The sex was good, somewhat surprisingly given that he was kind of nerdy. Gracie, drunk one night in the living room during the first party they'd thrown as roommates, leaned forward conspiratorially and whispered, her eyes wide, "You guys are going to have such beautiful babies. I love mixed babies." Dawn just laughed and said, "Okay," as Frances walked back into the room, holding two fresh beers from the fridge, and Gracie wheeled away across the living room to talk to some friends from the community theatre she volunteered at. Dawn watched Gracie for a moment as she mimed something for the group, who laughed and clapped their hands. Dawn turned back to Frances, who introduced her to a guy with a sour face and an incongruous head of soft, blond curls.

She continued to bartend and to date Frances, and the months passed by in a steady stream, though it was more than a stream, really; it was picking up debris and mud and silt as it went, swelling into this new shape of her life, becoming a flowing river, flowing along with Dawn bobbing in its current.

CHAPTER FIVE

D awn can't remember the last time there were this many people in the house, and there are only four of them, shuffling awkwardly to claim space in the cramped kitchen. Dawn stands next to the fridge, with a clear sightline to the front door, and Crystal and Mrs. Cleary stand in front of the sink, Crystal clasping and unclasping her hands in front of her.

Mrs. Cleary had appeared at the door with a giant cheese and broccoli casserole a few days after Dawn had inadvertently paid them a visit, and Martin had told her about Cody. "Won't it be nice for him to see some familiar faces? Crystal and I can help form the welcoming committee!" she'd declared.

Any minute now Dawn will witness her brother, a free man, walk through the front door. She hopes that they will embrace. That he won't hold her absence from the visiting room for seven years against her. That this freedom will be enough.

When the front door opens after an eternity of waiting, it is not her brother who walks through it. This man is tall and broad and dirty blond, wearing an old cracked leather vest. He looks like a biker—rough and mean but smiling. Rather, he's projecting a smile, like he wants everyone to believe he's friendly and relaxed.

Dawn feels a jolt, like an electric shock in her brain, like her nervous system producing a warning. But before she has time to decide what's behind the stranger's smile, Cody appears. He clasps a hand on the bigger man's shoulder and shuffles awkwardly past him in the narrow entryway. Cody strides into the kitchen, arms spread wide like he's blessing everyone. Then he wraps them tightly around himself, hugs himself, and begins to cry softly.

It is not the greeting that anyone expected, that's clear from the blank, slightly horrified looks on everyone's faces. Dawn has never seen Cody cry. The biker appears beside Cody and envelops him in his muscled arms.

Finally, unable to tolerate the sound of Cody quietly weeping any longer, Dawn says, "Cody? Are you…okay?"

She is keenly aware that this is the weakest possible response, but she has nothing else to offer. She has the disorienting feeling she's seen this before. That cold creep of certainty that something bad is about to happen. Like she knows how this part ends.

A few rattling, shaky breaths later, Cody gathers himself and raises his head, gently pushes the other man's arms away. He crosses to Dawn in two quick strides and hugs her. She smells sweat, cigarettes, some kind of cheap, strong deodorant, and under it all something else she can't identify during the few seconds her brother holds her tightly to him. Cody pulls away, looks at Dawn, and smiles, almost shyly. His eyes are dry and clear, like he hasn't been crying at all.

"Dawn! I can't...You can't know how good this feels, holy fuck." He shakes his head in disbelief.

Mrs. Cleary and Crystal both react subtly to Cody. His presence always registers in a room. He's had the same alternately compelling and repelling energy since high school.

Cody's eyes flick toward Crystal and Mrs. Cleary, still standing awkwardly in front of the sink, their smiles now determinedly fixed.

"Crystal, right?" he says, looking up at her on a very slight, almost imperceptible, angle, his dark lashes emphasized and brown eyes gone soft and inviting. That's the other thing about her brother—he's always been a dog.

"Yes!" Crystal almost yelps, she's so eager to break her and her mother's silence. "Cody, it's so...good to see you." She finishes pretty flat, but Dawn can't blame her.

"Sorry," Cody says, contrite and polite yet with that rangy hang to his limbs that is somehow evocative of a prison yard. "I can't remember your name, ma'am." He flashes a grin at Mrs. Cleary.

"That's all right, dear. It's Elena—Mrs. Cleary. So glad to see you again." She smiles and quickly nods her head a few times.

The stranger has yet to be introduced.

"Oh, right. Well, thanks for coming, Crystal and Mrs. Cleary. I was thinking we could all go out for supper. Like for steaks or something like that. I've been eatin' some pretty shit food the last little while!" Cody gives a hearty laugh like what he said was actually funny, and before anyone can respond, the biker steps forward.

"Hello everyone, my name's Tyler," he starts, like he's at an AA meeting. "And I'm good buds with Cody here. He's one of the best, I'll tell you that. A real beauty, this guy here." He smiles at Cody with what looks like genuine warmth, and Cody smiles back.

Martin is clutching a beer and nodding along fervently with Tyler's words.

"Anyway, thanks for having me in your home. It's a real honour and a privilege." Tyler grins around at everyone. "And if you'd all do me the favour of joining us for dinner tonight—well, I'd just really appreciate that. Cody's nearest and dearest, and all that."

Tyler looks like a biker, but talks like a used car salesman: all upfront, unrelenting charm with a greasy slick to it. The others seem like they're taken in by Tyler's little speech, and there's a general move to finish drinks, gather jackets and purses, and head toward the door, where Tyler stands, keys in hand, staring right at Dawn. She feels herself blush (*goddammit*) as their eyes meet but wills herself to hold his gaze for a few seconds.

Tyler smiles at her, a slow smile that doesn't reach his eyes, and for a moment, Dawn thinks she sees ... his face flicker. Like a bad connection. A shudder, a spasm of pain? Dawn has to look away, and Crystal is suddenly beside her. Crystal angles her small body toward Dawn, who momentarily feels huge and resists the urge to back away, put some distance between them.

Crystal leans in and says, "It must feel so good to have him home." She squeezes Dawn's limp hand between her two soft, hot ones, metallic turquoise nails forming a cage.

"Yes, it does," Dawn replies, even though she doesn't know what she feels—too much to parse it all, so much that it nulls out into nothing.

THE DRIVE TO the restaurant is quiet. Dawn and Martin ride together, and neither has any words for this situation. The night sky passes by the car windows, broken by the nonchalant ugliness of billboards and signs for the procession of strip malls. They pass the pizza place that has been there for Dawn's entire life and that she's never seen open or with any customers. They pass a billboard that is a photo grid of three women's faces, with the word MISSING in garish lettering next to them and a tip line to call with any information. The picture on the right shows a girl with wet-looking curls and dark eyeliner, staring defiantly out at the passing cars, the movements of the city below her.

The girl went missing after a party in an apartment building downtown. How many girls have walked into parties and bars expecting a fun night, or a dull one, expecting just another night out in a string of nights out, and found instead that it was their last one? Found instead that someone's evil eye was settling over them, from across the crowded room, from a passing car? This girl—the missing girl—was seen by several witnesses leaving the party alone, but she has not been seen by anyone since.

As Martin drives them past the billboard, Dawn imagines a procession of girls stepping into the night and being made to disappear. Dawn always wonders, with every new case, about the person who knows. How many cashiers, baristas, and waiters have served him, unknowing? It chills her to think of a young woman handing over his change, her fingers brushing his palm, and never thinking of him again—he's just another anonymous face in a line of customers.

The billboard recedes into the distance, but it stays with Dawn, a ghostly afterimage of its presence. Three more disembodied faces that most people forget as soon as they've driven past, because they believe that bad things like this do not touch them. Because they tell themselves that, somehow, those women were different. They must have been marked in some way, even done the marking themselves maybe—some people will go that far in their justifications. Dawn imagines the three faces that are not on the billboard. The three faces that may or may not be known—by someone who is too afraid or apathetic to talk, by authorities who don't care or can't act or bungled the investigation or waited too long.

Three missing women. Three people out there responsible for making them disappear.

For everyone damaged, a damager.

Dawn and Martin drive on in silence, a beautiful, blazing purple sunset above them. Dawn scrutinizes the faces of the people in the cars they pass, and wonders how much damage they've done in their lives. It's hard to calculate this grim mathematics, with time being the only reliable measure of its true extent. Survey the debris from across an expanse of years, and only then can you begin to quantify the pain, to see everything it took from you. Step back even further, and the destruction can last for generations.

When Dawn was nine years old there was a man caught in the city who had destroyed numerous lives. He was charged with the murder of three women who'd all been reported missing over the last few years. All three families of the missing women said the police didn't seem to be actively investigating the disappearances. There were no front-page headlines about the women while they were missing. The families were not asked to give press conferences pleading for a safe return. Only after he was caught were the three women front-page news, and only then because of what he did to them.

The newspaper always led with a glaring headline, and Dawn would watch Violet flip the paper over as she drifted through the kitchen. Violet refused to read the news stories or watch them on TV, changing the channel whenever the man's dead-eyed mug shot or the photos of the women, forever frozen in time, appeared on the screen.

Even back then, Dawn understood that her mother lived in fear of seeing a face she knew on the news one day, of receiving a call from someone who hadn't phoned in decades, only to bring unbearable news. When Dawn was younger, Violet told her once that she hadn't seen her own mother for twenty-five years, and they all knew that she had a rift with her sister from before her children even existed. Dawn never met her mother's mother, not even when she was little, and Violet's family had sometimes been around.

All the things Violet would never say, all the hurt she couldn't name and couldn't face, kept Dawn's mother from the world. Kept her separate. She seemed to her children like a woman divested from herself, adrift and strange. They knew so little of her, in the end. But then again, they did know the precise way her voice sounded, and the way her brow furrowed when she concentrated, the way her tongue flicked out to lick her lips. They knew the way she smelled—mineral and cool and like soap. Surely, that counted for something.

Dawn always knew that Violet loved her husband and her children fiercely, if distantly, but she also knew that Violet would walk away from the things she couldn't bear to see. From the things she'd seen already so many times.

So Dawn watched her mom flip over the newspapers.

But Dawn read the stories.

She learned that the man would wait until a storm hit, increasing the odds of a woman accepting his offer of a ride. He further increased those odds by bringing along his small son, whose presence must have reassured the women that he was a good, wholesome father, that they would be safe with him. Pale eyes behind glasses scanned the sidewalks and corners. Stubby fingers, wedding ring shiny and clearly visible, flicked restlessly through radio stations, snippets of pop songs cut off abruptly. And in the back seat, a little boy, bored, kicked his legs in the air and asked his dad what they were doing. Wheels rolled and rolled. Rain smacked the pavement. Wheels rolled gently to a stop.

The man was caught on a summer night, when the neighbour's insomniac son stepped out on the back porch to smoke a joint at three a.m. He heard the man digging under the big maple tree in his backyard and saw a vague shape in the dark, lying on the grass, that didn't look right. He dropped the joint, went inside, and called the police.

The perpetrator was a long-time manager at a local pharmacy. He had been married to his high school sweetheart for twelve years. An ordinary man, by all accounts. The evening news covered the story for a week, replaying the same interviews with a handful of friends, co-workers, neighbours. They all expressed shock, stressed how there were no signs of anything amiss. They all said:

"He was such a great guy."

"Great guy."

"Great guy."

"Great guy."

Dawn grew tired of the news anchors, who shook their heads solemnly and said, "It's such an unbelievable story," and then introduced the next segment, talked about a fundraiser for veterans and an upcoming agricultural fair, celebrated the twenty-fifth anniversary of a family-owned diner downtown. Then did it again the next night, until the women's story was dropped from the rotation. Of course, it wasn't really their story, and that was perhaps the final cruel twist; it was his story. He'd written them into his terrible narrative and then ended theirs. A particularly human barbarism.

The interest of the general population waned and let go, if it had ever been piqued to begin with, quickly swallowed up by the pall of indifference that hung over the city. These women weren't the right kind of women for the type of victimhood that inspired *Dateline* episodes and countless threads on Reddit. Strangers weren't haunted by the case; in fact, the rest of the country barely picked up the story. There were a few scattered national news reports and articles in the days immediately after the arrest, and then there was nothing. If he was remembered at all, the man would quickly become something other than a man. A beast, a monster, a devil, but the names would all mean the same thing—not human. Not just not *like* us, but not *of* us. In other words: not our problem. An abhorrent anomaly that couldn't have been foreseen. Unfixable, so why bother trying? Best not to look at it too closely.

What was so confounding about the fact of an ordinary

man's violence? So many people needed monsters to look monstrous. They couldn't accept, despite all the evidence to the contrary, that the demons looked just like them. That a seemingly regular life could conceal a deeply vicious soul.

The women's purses and shoes were found in a cardboard box with mould growing along the waterlogged flaps, shoved to the back of the garage. It wasn't particularly well hidden for the years it sat there, collecting rain runoff and dust. The man's wife later said she didn't notice the box or its contents—she rarely even entered the garage. "That's his space," she said.

The son was whisked away by his mother, quickly and quietly, to her hometown in British Columbia, and there was nothing more reported about him. Dawn wondered what the boy looked like, but there were no photos of him because he was five years old when his father committed his crimes with him in the back seat. She wasn't interested in the colour of his hair or how his body was built—she was curious to know what expression could be read in his eyes. She could only ever imagine a vaguely defined little boy, a smudge of brown hair over a pale face, with eyes stunned to blankness. And within that vacuum, what would take hold?

She knew already by then that absence was not the presence of nothing; it was the phantom presence of someone who had gone. Or had been taken. Absence begets absence—a life was taken, and those left behind were taken from, too. The shock waves reached out and out and out, until everyone was unsteady on their feet.

Dawn thought that, surely, everyone in this city should be quaking, struggling to keep their footing. She started to resent those who could still walk steady here, and that resentment took hold in her, wormed its way deep inside her and latched on.

THE PARKING LOT of the Italian restaurant is nearly empty, with only a few scattered cars in the large parking lot. The air is chilly when they step out of the car. It's still too early for snow, but it won't be long now until the city starts its dance with winter; the first snowfall won't last, will melt away when the temperatures climb slightly again, to be replaced, finally, with the real thing: a thick layer muffling the frozen ground for months.

"Someone's burnin' something," Martin remarks, and inhales deeply.

Dawn ignores him as they shuffle toward the restaurant; anxiety is humming through her whole body now, making it hard to speak. Martin's eyes are moist, as though he's on the verge of tears of joy, and there is an undeniable bounce in his step. Seeing him this happy brings his depression into clearer focus, the depths to which he'd sunk while Cody was away illuminated by his new-found joy. Dawn wants him to be happy. She does.

She holds the door open for her dad and follows him inside, into a wall of heat. The restaurant is toasty. Dawn sheds her parka as they head over to the table the others have claimed. There are only three other occupied tables.

Dawn ends up in the empty seat between Cody and Tyler along one side of the table. She glances at the two men before asking, forced cheer in her voice, "So, how do you two know each other anyway?"

Cody and Tyler look at each other and chuckle, like they're remembering the same funny story.

"Well!" Tyler's laugh is coarse and booming. "I guess you could say we met through the prison. I teach a coding class there every week. Computers—" he wiggles his fingers in the air over an invisible keyboard. Dawn tries to catch Cody's eye as Tyler talks, but he won't look at her. "Cody was a student in his first year of bein' incarcerated and we became friends. I got him into some more advanced online coding courses once he finished my little intro course—with top grades, I might add! I volunteered to supervise him and a coupla other boys while they did these online courses. Was the least I could do."

The whole table is rapt under Tyler's spell. Except Dawn, who keeps getting distracted by a flickering light behind Tyler near the back of the dining area. It's throwing crazy shadows up the fading floral wallpaper and—Dawn squints—is it *swinging,* too?

An unusual noise is coming from … the kitchen? A low buzzing, or a quiet mechanical chittering. Heat creeps up her throat as though its source is her stomach and not the restaurant's blasting HVAC. The temperature is overwhelming. The skin on Dawn's face constricts. She looks around desperately at the others, but they're all listening intently to Tyler, still talking, with expansive hand gestures and glittering eyes.

Dawn grabs the water glass in front of her and chugs it down. The buzzing fills her ears with an almost physical pressure. She wonders if her skin is red and boiled-looking, if wisps of steam are rising from her body. Her tongue feels bloated and she has to unstick it from the roof of her mouth to speak; she needs to speak, a flame licking up from her core, the restaurant about to blow open, that awful sound reaching a fever pitch—

And then, like snapping suddenly out of a hallucination, the sound falls away and the table comes back into focus and the suffocating heat subsides.

Dawn pats the front of her shirt; she's not even sweating. She watches Martin take his toque off across from her and lay it on the table, notices there's still a chill clinging to her clothes.

Something's moving, she thinks.

Maybe this thing started a long time ago and is only now catching up to her. Or maybe it's not about her at all.

She wolfs down her fettucine alfredo and garlic toast, watches Cody shift spaghetti bolognese around on his plate. Tyler and Cody continue talking, telling stories like they just got back from a long, adventurous trip together. Crystal stares at Cody, enthralled. Everything is wrapped up in Cody, filtered through Cody—the thing that looms behind every action, every feeling, every discussion, that forces itself to be considered, always.

Dawn downs her glass of too-sweet, room-temperature wine. *What's going on here, brother?*

CHAPTER SIX

TORONTO

Gracie threw her arms around Dawn, the scent of the thick coconut oil she liberally rubbed in every evening rising from her warm skin. It was a long, hard hug, the kind that still felt awkward to Dawn, even after two years of trying to adjust to Gracie's easy, friendly physicality. Dawn told herself to squeeze back, to relax. She would miss bingeing *The Real Housewives* together, and her roommate's cheerful chatter while she flitted from cutting board to stove doing most of the prepping and cooking for one of their household dinners Grace named *Family Nights*.

"I'll miss you crazy kids!" Gracie embraced Frances next, who smiled his slow, shy smile at Dawn over Gracie's petite shoulder.

Casey appeared in the doorway in slippers and a tatty

robe, exuding the stale musk of a hangover. She gave them both sleepy one-armed hugs and told them not to be strangers, strangers.

Frances and Dawn were moving in together. The landlord had told them all a month ago that he planned on renovating their main floor/basement unit, so they had thirty days to move out. It had become a common ploy in the city for landlords who wanted to jack up the rent on their shitty units without doing much work. Disgruntled and drunk after the announcement, Casey declared the landlord would probably redo the tiles in one bathroom, and then put the whole thing back on the market for thousands more than they'd paid. She went on a long, meandering rant about tenants' and squatters' rights that none of them paid attention to. Defiantly, she wrenched the metal toilet-paper holder off the wall in the basement bathroom and threw it into the weedy backyard. They watched it arc through the air and vanish as it landed somewhere in the dark mass of vegetation. Casey whirled around to give the middle finger to the landlord's upstairs window, then tripped and fell off the edge of the porch. They all ended the night sprawled on the two couches shoved into the living room, singing a horrendous a cappella version of "Auld Lang Syne," Casey's knee propped up by a pack of frozen berries.

Two nights after the announcement, as they lay in bed together watching a very bad animated movie about a family of monkeys, Frances turned to Dawn and asked if she wanted to move in together. His question was breathless and rushed, completely devoid of elegance or romance. Dawn said, "Yes, of course," and kissed him.

Gracie and Casey were sticking together, too. They'd found an apartment all their friends were deeply jealous of—a cute place with original hardwood floors, white wainscotting, and a tiny but private backyard. Dawn and Frances were moving into one of the new grey-and-glass towers of a mini-complex close by. Their building was thirty storeys. It stood next to an identical building, and two others across the way completed the site, with an un-landscaped courtyard in between. It certainly wasn't beautiful, but at least it was new. Old buildings meant drafts and no A/C and bugs. Dawn wanted new.

On the day of their departure, Dawn and Frances waved like they were going away to sea, as they walked backwards down the sidewalk. The pageantry of the farewell felt good. It was summertime and the big trees were reaching for each other's canopies, the street shielded beneath them in a dappling of shadow and golden light. They held hands as they walked toward the streetcar stop. This feeling of lightness, of things flowing easily, was unfamiliar to Dawn, and underneath her contentment was a current of distrust.

Their condo was on the seventeenth floor and the elevators, despite there being four of them, were excruciatingly slow. Dawn practised breathing techniques that she'd googled, told herself it was dumb to be annoyed by something she couldn't control. But she was still annoyed, every day, by the elevators. The walls of their place were thinner than she would have liked and their neighbours louder.

Partially in order to help drown out said neighbours, they usually had music playing, not too loud, a background hum that could be tuned in or out of as they desired, something Dawn felt like she could get used to. As they got ready for dinner one night a few months after they'd moved in, the throbbing bass from their next-door neighbour's techno mix somewhat spoiled the charm of the radio show Frances had on, one that spotlighted emerging Canadian musicians.

"It just means the company can't profit—the profits go back into running it? Like, there's no owner who can get rich. Employees can still make a lot of money—like with the big festivals and stuff. But you need to be really high up for that," Frances explained as he chopped perfectly uniform peppers for the quinoa salad (reading it off the house shopping list for the first time, Dawn had pronounced it *ke-noah*, and all the roommates laughed, except for Frances).

"Guess I'll just have to work my way up!" Dawn trilled. She could hardly believe she had an interview next week—the first interview she'd gotten in the past six months of applying for jobs outside of serving, urged on by an encouraging Frances, who sent her job postings on Facebook Messenger while he was at the university during the day and followed up with her in the evening when he got home. She'd applied to them all but had never heard back. Until now.

She sat on the end of their bed and watched Frances

make dinner. She'd initially appreciated his orderliness, his careful and deliberate preparations—how every action had a proper order in which it should be completed, and how he followed this order meticulously. However, recently, this quality had sometimes begun to prickle at her. He was this way whether he was making dinner, fixing his bike, or having sex. This last was the area where Dawn had become least appreciative. What had been a welcome novelty (it wasn't that he was bad at things, just that it was always the same things, in the same way) when they'd first started going out was now growing tedious.

Frances smiled at her and said, "Why don't you get through the interview first?"

This was another habit of his Dawn didn't like, this dancing around the matter. The way he used a smile to conceal the meaning of his words. In this case, that she might not even get hired. That she might not be good enough to be hired. But he hadn't said that straight out; instead, he was hiding it with a smile and tepid, throwaway words.

Sun was streaming in through the glass balcony door (it opened onto a tiny cement square, barely big enough for Dawn and Frances to stand on at the same time—a definite downgrade from the backyard at the shared house, but it still counted as outdoor space) and lay in golden streaks across the fake wood flooring. It warmed Dawn, not physically because it wasn't touching her, but, still, she felt warmer toward Frances's stupid way of avoiding saying things directly. She felt a rush of pleasure—the condo, their new place together, was admittedly tight for two people, but Dawn loved it. Loved its newness, its cleanness, its modern, straight lines. Loved the clean white bathtub without a rusted ring of dirt that she could sink down into, luxuriate in, and feel the perspiration bead and drip down the back of her neck, her mass of brown hair gathered up in a bun becoming slick with sweat. She liked to stay in the bath until her skin was flushed red and the sweat trickled unignorably into her eyes.

She leaned into the pleasure and pushed away her lingering annoyance. She got up from the bed, walked the few steps to where Frances stood at the counter, and wrapped her arms around him from behind, something she still savoured—this casual but intense intimacy that she'd never had before with a man, that she'd never wanted before with any man she'd known. It seemed a world removed from the physicality she'd shared with a series of uninspiring, ambitionless boys in her hometown who'd slept on bare mattresses on the floor in their parents' basements and driven beaters that smelled like cigarettes and fast food. Boys who felt no particular need to get out of that place, who shrugged and said they liked it there, where else would they go? if she ever ventured to bring it up.

Frances was the stark opposite of those boys waning away in their childhood homes. He was smart and dedicated, finishing up his degree after seven long years. He wanted to be a history professor once he'd gotten his PhD. The appeal of spending that long studying was lost on Dawn, but she admired his dedication. He looked at Dawn like she was something beautiful and surprising, sometimes randomly reached out and tucked her hair behind her ear.

She pressed her face into Frances's back, bending slightly because she was about an inch taller than him, and pressed her cheekbone against his shoulder blade through his cotton-blend T-shirt, breathed in the smell of him. His arm slowed then stopped chopping the vegetables, and he placed his hands over hers, wrapped around his midsection, and squeezed them gently. They stayed like that until their breathing matched up, until their bodies found each other's rhythm, and then he turned around and cupped her face and kissed her, soft, then intense, urgent. She felt his dick press hard against her and wondered, quickly, briefly, if she smelled bad right then, but then his hand moved up to her breast, and she tried to lose herself, tried hard to allow herself to be lost in the routine, as they tumbled together onto the bed.

THE NIGHT BEFORE Dawn started her new job at the not-for-profit art centre, she woke from a nightmare, her body shaking next to Frances's relaxed, still form. She shifted away, afraid to contaminate him with her fear, and faced the blank white wall of their bedroom.

A dark hallway shimmered and faded into a snowy back lane, trembled and became the wall again, became the back lane. A clicking, a whirring, engulfed Dawn. Some great, alien machine was calling out to her.

CHAPTER SEVEN

After dinner, Mrs. Cleary and Crystal both beg off. Mrs. Cleary cites her arthritic hip, and Crystal wants to get home to say goodnight to her boys. She shows them a few pictures on her phone before leaving—three blond blurs that are Crystal and the boys splashing in a pool, the kids flashing gap-toothed grins as they hold up complex-looking military tank toys, Jake and the detritus of Christmas wrapping paper in the background.

Dawn expects Tyler to make his exit as well, but instead he rides back home with them, his long legs pressing into Dawn's back. She'll be damned if she gives him the front. She does not move her seat up.

When they get back to the house, Martin retires for the night and leaves their trio standing in the kitchen. Tyler plunks into a chair like he's been there a thousand times before, and Cody rummages in the fridge for beer. Dawn looks over his shoulder to see if there's any wine.

When she turns, Tyler's eyes are fixed on her. A strange man's eyes on her body (and sometimes a familiar one's) produce a creeping, crawling feeling. The certainty of possession in the gaze is, in the moment, akin to possession. Their looks fleetingly possess her body, its contours, where it hangs heavy, where it curves, and where it dips. Her body becomes a burden to her under these gazes.

Cody hands her a half-empty bottle of white wine and pulls three beers hanging off a plastic six-pack ring out from behind some condiments. The wine is on the edge of being spoiled, but Dawn drinks it anyway, cold and sour on her tongue.

Cody leans forward over the table and looks Dawn, and then Tyler, in the eyes. "It feels amazing," he says. "To be out. You can't imagine how amazing."

Dawn doesn't know how to respond. The gulf between them opens before her, too wide to cross. She can't even see the outline of his figure on that other, distant, shore. Dawn wishes she could talk to her brother alone. She wants to ask him how he is, how he really is.

You've had seven years to ask him that, she chides herself.

"I'm glad you're home," she says, because there's nothing else to say. This place is home for neither of them, not anymore. Dawn doesn't have a home to go back to in

Toronto, and Cody hasn't had the chance to make a home of his own yet. So they're alike in that way—adrift.

"Thank you, sis," Cody says.

He's never called her *sis*. She smiles and sips her drink.

"What's your story?" Tyler grins wolfishly across the table at her. "Sis."

Dawn wills the heat of her anger down. Where does it go when it's stamped down so expertly, when it isn't released?

"My story? Like, what?" She knows it doesn't really matter, but giving any ground feels like losing the war right now, even if it's a war only she's fighting.

"Like…where do you live? What do you do? How long are you staying here for?"

And with that, Dawn realizes that, of course, Cody and Tyler didn't know she'd be here. She's a surprise.

"I live in Toronto. Well, I used to. But I'm staying here for a bit…you know, to help Dad out. I think…he gets lonely."

"Cool, cool." Tyler nods smoothly. "How'd Toronto treat you? Haven't been that way in a few years myself."

"I got a bit bored of it," she replies. "I loved it at first, but…I got homesick, I guess." She takes a big gulp of wine.

Cody is nodding and smiling along to her story. "That's right, that's right," he affirms. "Fuckin' A. Never liked that place."

"You've never been!" Dawn laughs, and Cody flicks moisture from his beer bottle at her.

"Read about it, though! Never liked it." He laughs the same uproarious, barking laugh he had as a teen, and Dawn is shot through with the sweetest bitter nostalgia. A physical pressure crushing the cage of her chest. She can't bear it. Remembering her brother as a boy, as a young adult—she can't quite square her memories with the man before her. She downs the rest of the wine and gets up, mumbling about being tired.

Her room is cold, but she hardly feels it. She lies on her back on top of the covers and stares at the dark ceiling, the shifting shadows. Being back here is not good for her. Too many memories, rushing in. Rushing in.

She didn't attend her high school graduation ceremony or the safe grad party thrown by their school that corralled everyone into a room in the convention centre downtown, patrolled relentlessly by parent volunteers. After a banquet-style dinner of bland food for students and their families, the students were allowed to get shit-faced as long as they were picked up by their designated guardians at the end of the night. She received her diploma in the mail a week later and didn't bother to open it. Her high school years held few, if any, fond memories—a pale drift of smoke, hard to see clearly and passed in a haze. She'd put the manila envelope with a stack of magazines in the living room and forgotten about it.

Yet graduation did shake something alive in Dawn, and she started to want to be around people again. Maybe staring down the blank road of her looming future jogged some primal instinct for survival—or at least human interaction—deep within her. That was also when Violet started to come to her with more frequency, and for years, Dawn wondered if it was her longing for company that inspired these visitations from her mother, these hauntings. Dawn wasn't sure what to call the fleeting moments when her mother, or at least her voice, was suddenly, briefly, with her again. Sometimes these moments deeply frightened Dawn, yet it was still comforting to know that some part of Violet, somehow, still existed somewhere.

Violet came to Dawn in the bodies of others, in the daytime and at night. She came for seconds at a time, appeared and then vanished, leaving the people she spoke through unaware that anything had happened. One man with his hands casually in his pockets turned to Dawn on the street and spoke without breaking stride. At the sound of Violet's quiet rasp, at once gentle and abrasive, emanating so improbably from another human being, Dawn would suddenly be pinned to the past, a girl standing outside her mother's bedroom door, thinking about how her collarbones looked like sharp wings. She wanted to unstick herself from that moment, wanted a different memory to flood her in its place, but this was always where she was taken first. She wasn't sure that she knew how to miss her mother properly; so many memories bore the sharp sting of pain. But the sound of her mother's voice also brought hope, though Dawn knew deep down that it was a futile hope. She hoped each time, after the initial shock had worn off, often as she stood staring after whoever had spoken, that Violet would actually appear, not just her voice, and, even more impossibly, that she would stay. That her mother would be here with her again, silent and strange, but Dawn wouldn't mind it so much this time. It wouldn't matter so much this time if only Violet would come back.

For a long time, Dawn kept track of the words that people spoke to her in her dead mother's voice, wrote them down in a black-and-white marble-covered notebook she kept in the drawer of her bedside table, alongside the random assortment of loose condoms, receipts, movie ticket stubs, and an old necklace, hopelessly tangled, its cheap metal green in places.

Eventually, she stopped recording them, unable to find a pattern or meaning in the words.

Dawn drifted through the languid days after graduating, set loose into the summer. But her loneliness clawed her awake at night. Cody would bring friends home once in a while, when Martin was on the road, and they'd stay up late, smoking inside and talking loudly in the living room. Dawn didn't hang out with them. She wore earplugs on these occasions, drowning them out pretty successfully, except when a fight broke out.

One night, she woke to a huge crash that she learned the next day was their coffee table exploding under the body-slammed weight of Cody's friend Chris. The next day, she and Cody took the debris to the dump, piling it into the back seat of their shared Toyota, driving in silence because Dawn was freezing Cody out, tired of the bullshit that eternally surrounded him. On the ride back, Cody steered them to the McDonald's drive-through and bought Dawn a combo meal as a peace offering. When they got home, Dawn went straight to her room to escape the stench of stale smoke and beer. Martin didn't notice the missing coffee table when he got back a few days later.

Finally, not much later, Dawn gave in to the silent battle she'd been fighting with herself and asked her brother if she could go with him to play pool.

She remembers Cody standing in the back lot of the pool hall, under the buttery light of a street lamp, blowing a cloud of smoke into the humid summer air, sticky and close even at night. The heat wave that summer was relentless, a cloak over everything and everyone. He passed Dawn the smoke and she took a few drags before dropping it on the gravel. They headed back inside, through the back door that was propped open with a brick, down a short dark hallway, and into a big square room with pool tables lining the perimeter and a circular bar in the middle. Fluorescent lights swayed lazily on their cords, and the carpet was thin and rough, decades of spilled alcohol soaked into its fibres.

A couple of grizzled old-timers sat at the bar most nights, steadily downing whisky and Cokes, talking to anyone who came to order drinks. One of them, Jerry, lit up whenever he saw Dawn and called her *Sugar*, always offered to buy her a shot. Occasionally, she accepted. Jerry looked like he lived hard—lined face, yellowing white beard, deeply callused hands. Sometimes Jerry got so drunk he fell asleep on his bar stool, his head tilting onto his doughy chest, emitting rattling snores that sounded like they hurt. Sometimes Jerry cried when he talked to Dawn, tears leaking from his red eyes.

Cody and his friends—now maybe also Dawn's friends—hung out at the pool hall a lot. The drinks and the pool were cheap, so it was a good place to start the nights that inevitably ended in Chris's West End apartment in a six-storey building of pale limestone and brick on the corner of a busy road and a residential street. His apartment's decor was sparse, featuring a mishmash of chunky old furniture, rickety IKEA builds, and velvet black-light posters on the walls. Chris had a bookcase full of DVDs and insisted on always playing a movie in the background, constantly rattling off film trivia. Dawn guessed he was a few years older than Cody. He had thin, sloping shoulders, and he was always moving—rolling joints with surprisingly elegant fingers, tapping his foot, shaking his leg, gesturing with his arms and hands as he spoke.

As Dawn spent more time with Cody and his friends, she noticed that the dynamic between her brother and Chris wasn't always harmonious. They often, in fact, seemed to be subtly clashing—arguing, unjustly heatedly, about which *Expendables* actor was the toughest, disagreeing on pizza toppings. Stupid things.

Her brother was more combative in general. He was quicker to anger and didn't laugh as easily or as freely as he used to, biting back his laughter like he shouldn't have allowed himself to relax in this way. His face looked hard—closed off and impenetrable—and Dawn would find herself searching for a sign of softness or tenderness. But his face and body was often just one sign—a warning to others not to approach.

When Dawn thinks of him as a teenager, she imagines that he must have looked out over the fields at the edge of South Saint Jude, where the area tapers off into undeveloped prairie, and seen not abundance but emptiness. He was never able to feel whole in this place. She knows what that feels like. The fields echoed the emptiness between his ribs, in the pit of his belly. Empty all the way through.

When Cody was nineteen, he spent a lot of time in the in-between spaces of young men transitioning to adulthood. Parents' basements, some half-finished and dank and unwelcoming, others converted into semi-suites. The one-bedroom apartments of some of his friends were depressing in their sameness—cheap, ill-kept units in buildings with broken front door locks. Baseball bats kept in the bedroom. Cody had convinced Chris to buy some of the old-school velvet black-light paintings from the head shop run by an old hippie downtown. They would sit in the dark, blasted on speedy pressed-tabs of E, smoking Chris's sloppily rolled joints, and watch the thinly glowing paintings—pinks and greens and yellows tracing together, pulsing. They looked dull and sad in the morning, though, and the black light broke shortly after they bought it.

Chris's apartment became the de facto hangout spot after Cody got in a drunken fight with an older regular at the pool hall. Cody smashed the guy's nose and maybe his jaw, and this was certainly enough to be banned from the quiet bar.

Dawn can't pinpoint exactly when she stopped denying Cody's rage to herself and started worrying about it. Worrying about his tightly coiled energy, his turbulent moods that could influence a room full of people, could make even her turn her eyes away—not so much in fear, but because she didn't want to deal with the aftermath of setting him off. It's a rage she also knows; it runs through the middle of her, a deep and lonely river that rises to the surface, unbidden. She fights not to lose herself in its waters because she fears what might happen if she does. It's a dangerous feeling, a feeling with no limit, this fear of giving herself over to it.

By the time Cody was twenty, he and his buddies had taken to hanging around in the parking lot of Chris's building as much as they did indoors, the neighbours becoming less and less tolerant of the noise, the smoke, the occasional fight. It was on one of these outdoor nights that it happened.

After the guy from the end of the hallway, who was wild-eyed and keyed-up, came to the door and yelled (improbably) about needing to sleep, Chris kicked them out, and they decamped to a corner of the building's back parking lot to finish their beer. Throughout that hot summer, they pressed the cold beers against their sweaty arms and necks until the bottles were warm. A back lane ran beside the parking lot, separated by a low fence that was easy to jump over, just wooden pylons with chains slung barely above the ground between them. The lane followed the backs of clapboard houses crammed close together on tiny lots, some leaning intimately toward their neighbours as though about to steal a clandestine kiss in the dark.

That night, a figure walked toward their small group, emerging from around the bend in the back lane, a slight slope to his lanky frame. There were only a few of them left and it was getting late. Dawn remembers spitting out her last mouthful of warm beer onto the pavement as they got ready to leave. She wondered if Cody was going to slip off elsewhere to sleep or take the bus home with her. She wants to remember what day of the week it was; she wants to remember every detail precisely, as though a clearly articulated set of facts would help to make things make sense.

The figure approached them with a noticeable swerve, not a swagger but a drunken sway. Once the figure got close enough to the light, Dawn saw that he was younger than she thought. He was wearing black jeans, black sneakers, and some death metal band's T-shirt that caused their friend Richard to call out, "Hey man, nice shirt!" The stranger responded by smiling, closing his eyes, and drunkenly raising a celebratory fist in the air. The other fist was clutching a forty of Jack Daniel's, the plastic seal still wrapped around the cap.

After that initial encounter, he appeared in the back lane more and more often, and it wasn't long before he was invited up to Chris's apartment. His name was Jeremy and he lived down the lane from the apartment building with his mom, who worked night shifts as an ER triage nurse, and his stepdad, who spent most nights drinking himself through anger to belligerence to incoherence to passing out. It didn't take long for them to learn these details because Jeremy was usually very drunk and always very talkative, delivering a flat-out confessional stream once he reached a certain tipping point in the night. The guys in their group felt slightly bad for him and definitely enjoyed the booze he regularly took from his parents and always shared. From one beer to the next, Jeremy would start slurring his words. He would make advances on the girls in their group that were so sloppy, reaching out a hand here or there, the girls didn't even have to push him away, just sidestep him or walk off.

When Dawn thinks back, lying on her bed and staring up at the shadows playing on the ceiling, she can't remember Cody ever talking to Jeremy for any length of time; she can only picture them at opposite ends of the room, engaged in separate conversations, Cody smoking with whatever girl he had hanging around, Jeremy probably sitting by Chris, who was the one who tolerated him the most. She searches her memory but can't come up with a single one of Cody and Jeremy hanging out with each other. She wishes she knew if this were true, like she wishes she knew if they first met Jeremy on a Tuesday or a Wednesday. The facts and the truth dance around each other, but no matter how hard she tries, she can't put them in an order that leads to understanding.

CHAPTER EIGHT

TORONTO

Dawn was fifteen minutes late for her first day of work, tripped up by the city's infuriatingly slow and overcrowded transit system. Three packed-to-the-brim streetcars passed her as she seethed, desperately checked the time on her phone. After she was finally able to get on a car, she ended up running the three blocks from the stop and was breathing heavily when she arrived at the front doors of the centre. She searched for the name of the place—United Arts for Change—on the intercom next to the door, found it, and pressed the buzzer. The art centre was in a tall light-brick building downtown ("a *heritage* building," emphasized June, the woman who had interviewed and hired Dawn) that housed a hodgepodge of businesses, art galleries, and artist studios.

The galleries in the building seemed humble and hearty, particularly in comparison to Dawn's most recent gallery experience. Frances and her former roommates had assured her that their friend's performance piece would be worth the trip to the waterfront. The performance and accompanying art exhibit were held in a cavernous warehouse space ("a pop-up gallery!" they proclaimed) by the lakeshore. A huge man stood by the door (*Galleries need bouncers?*) stamping hands after people paid the ten-dollar cover. Dawn wandered into the immense space, the ceilings disappearing into a murkiness of beams.

"Is this place, like, up to code? It doesn't look very safe," she asked warily.

Casey and Gracie exchanged a little look and nudged her. "Don't be such a Debbie Downer!" Gracie exclaimed.

Dawn smiled and hoped some rusty metal thing wouldn't fall on her head and brain her while she was taking in the art.

Frances passed her a small plastic cup of shitty red wine, dispensed by two girls who looked like BDSM models— both wore leather kilts and leather bras, one with short spiky red hair and the other with platinum blond braids that fell fetchingly over her breasts, which were pushed out and outlined by the straps of her halter, her nipples covered with black, star-shaped stickers. Dawn was surprised by how many middle-aged people there were in the crowd, mingling with the teens and twenty- and thirtysomethings like they belonged. And who was Dawn to say they didn't? Frances was so thrilled at the prospect of bringing her here, of giving her "an experience outside of what you're accustomed to," that she was determined not to seem like a tragic bumpkin.

Frances pulled her away from the series of poorly executed pen-and-ink drawings suspended from wires of vague forms that suggested female nudes, the only clearly discernible features luridly oversized breasts and lips that she'd been looking at, frowning, and brought her toward the circle that had formed in the middle of the space.

In the centre of the circle stood the friend, the promised performer, dressed in what looked to Dawn like flowing white rags with fringe. The performance involved a lot of slow swaying, gyrations gradually sped up to match the heavy synth track that blared from a concealed speaker system. It culminated with the woman, long blond hair whirling as she twisted and flailed, producing a used tampon from the folds of her rags, which she laid reverently on the floor, then crouched over, Gollum-esque. She enclosed the tampon with her body, forming a dome of bony back, and pressed her forehead to the warehouse floor.

The crowd erupted in rapturous applause. Dawn clapped along and smiled back at Frances, who was clapping with enthusiasm, eyes lit up.

"That performance was so, so good! It really spoke to like … the empowerment of women's bodies," Casey said as they left the warehouse / gallery. The night air had a chill to it, down by the water.

"But those awful drawings! I can't believe they exhibited them. So... racist! The way they sexualized the Black female form?" Gracie offered as they crowded together against the wind and Frances called an Uber.

"Totally. The girl I'm seeing is Caribbean," Casey contributed. "She hates that shit."

Pressed against the door of the car, Dawn held Frances's hand in the back seat, and he traced indecipherable patterns along her clammy palm as he animatedly joined the discussion. Dawn pressed her forehead against the cool glass of the window, watched cars and cyclists stream by, and allowed the wine sloshing in her bloodstream to empty her head, to take her away, to erase all the sounds and sights around her and leave her in that blank place, where no one else could go.

At the art centre, Dawn was now quickly buzzed in, the chipper voice that greeted her, crackling and oddly distorted over the intercom ("Come in, Dawn! Come in!") unmistakably June's.

Dawn pulled open the front door of the heritage building and stepped into a modern, newly renovated lobby. The light from the tall, wide windows bounced off the shiny floor and created a dazzling effect, like light refracting off a crystal. Huge, lushly green plants, their pots six feet around, stretched toward the ceiling in all the corners, while tasteful black leather couches with chrome details clustered in groups around small, unobtrusive tables dotted around the area, creating semi-private (or at least the illusion of semi-private) meeting areas.

Dawn headed for the elevators at the back of the lobby, which gleamed so intensely she felt dirty just looking at them. *How often do they clean in here?* she wondered, as she used a knuckle to press the Up button, not wanting to leave behind a vulgar fingerprint on the spotless chrome.

When the doors slid open, there was a woman in the back-left corner of the roomy elevator. She was standing very straight and rigid, pinched into the corner despite the rest of the elevator being empty. She was staring straight at Dawn. As the doors had opened, she was already looking into Dawn's eyes, a piercing gaze like a skewer. Abruptly, the woman's eyes flicked down and away. Dawn stepped into the elevator as though she were under water, in slow motion, floating forward. She stepped into the elevator despite the panicked thrumming of her heart. Her mouth tasted dry and faintly salty.

As the doors slid closed, Dawn realized the woman beside her was crying with no sound. The woman hunched forward and down in convulsive movements, weeping uncontrollably but silently. A sound like metal on metal—scraping—began to rise around them. Dawn didn't remember pushing the button for the third floor, but suddenly they were there; the doors were sliding open, the 3 button was lit up, and the woman was turning and looking up at Dawn from her hunched over position, and Dawn moved forward, moved through the doors, and looked back at the woman, who was moving her chapped mouth with no sound, working her jaw, foam frothing in the corners of her lips, and that grinding sound was still rising, and finally she rasped, "Dawn."

Urgent and afraid, it was Violet's voice.

DAWN ROUNDS A TURN in the back lane as the cold bite in the air lodges deep in her lungs' tissues with every panting breath. Her heart beats so forcefully she fears it might stop, might batter and bruise itself against her ribs until it gives out.

Dawn rounds the corner of the narrow back lane and there they are. Tail lights cast an artificial red glow on a garage door, a cop car parked askew. She pulls up short on the icy, frozen snow. She doesn't want to go any closer. The police are minutes, or seconds, away from turning down the lane from the other end, sirens wailing. She only sees them for a few seconds.

She is running down the back lane, running toward the moment that everything else branches out from. But—is that true? Time is not a flat, linear line but an impossibly complex pattern, turning and changing and folding over itself, a kaleidoscope.

Dawn is standing in a backyard under a maple tree, its barren branches disappearing into a black sky, freshly turned earth gently engulfing her feet. A bird or insect gives a strange cry from somewhere high in the branches.

She knows this place.

She sinks to her knees and cries out, but her voice is not her voice but a peculiar, incessant buzzing. The sound vibrates in her mouth, her throat, rattles her teeth as it pours forth. She fears she will choke, but, somehow, she doesn't. She continues to cry, the dirt soft beneath her knees.

DAWN JERKED BACK to herself standing stock-still facing the closed elevator doors. Her legs were shaking so hard she had to lean against the wall to steady herself. She pinched the soft skin of her underarm over and over, the sharp bursts of pain bringing her back to the world.

There was nothing to do but to keep moving forward.

She set off down the hall for the first day of her new job.

June gave Dawn a tour of the centre, which was several offices and conference rooms off a long hallway that opened into a common lounge area/art space and kitchen. The common area had a few worn-looking brown couches and armchairs at one end and large circular tables set up at the other for art projects and eating. Behind the couches there was a big supply cupboard, kept locked. The last two rooms were where the classes—"workshops," June called them— happened with the youth who dropped in after school, a rotating cast with a few regular characters, Dawn would soon discover. They did not, as a whole, particularly enjoy the workshops, but Dawn would notice that kids would come back, evening after evening, weekend after weekend (at least for a stretch), and would seem to be able to, perhaps for the first time that day, relax. So that was something.

Different instructors came to teach the workshops for a few weeks at a time, and each staff member had to commit to teaching a workshop, which June told Dawn after she was hired. The youth also used the large stainless-steel kitchen at the back of the space for cooking classes—a "life skills workshop"—though Dawn struggled to categorize cooking spaghetti as a life skill.

The tour concluded back at one of the offices, a square, uninspired room with two desks and large windows.

"And you'll be working in here with me!" June swept her arm around the room as if indicating a grand prize won on a game show.

Dawn smiled, acknowledging the offering. "Looks great," she said, because she wasn't the type of person to say anything more than that. Small talk didn't come easily. She wasn't sure how to connect with June, who was palpably eager for this to happen.

For a fraction of a second, June's face faltered, almost indiscernibly, before her smile picked itself back up again. "This one's yours." She indicated the desk to the right, plain faux-blond wood, neat and clean and new-looking, dominated by a desktop Mac. "Once we get you logged in to your email, there should be a welcome message from HR, some documents to review, that kind of thing."

Dawn nodded like she knew what documents June was talking about. She'd already signed the contract. She would learn later that the contract didn't matter nearly as much as she thought, that you could still just up and leave if that's what you chose to do.

June asked her if she knew how to log into Gmail and Dawn said that she did, hoping to keep the insult out of her voice.

"Some of the kids don't. They don't have email accounts," June said tragically, her mouth pulling down in a frown.

Dawn could only think to say, "I ... have a Gmail account."

Anxiety burst in Dawn's chest as she entered the login information for her new work email, copying it from a neon-green Post-it June was holding out in front of her. Dawn couldn't stop glancing at June's fingers on the paper, her nails thick and square and large.

Dawn's inbox appeared on the screen, an email from Cassandra in HR waiting for her. June was still standing beside her; Dawn expected her to excuse herself now, move over to her own desk, and leave Dawn to at least figure out what documents she was supposed to read. Dawn wasn't sure what to do. Should she open the email and start reading anyway?

"Dawn, I'd like to tell you a bit about our organization, a bit of information about us. Our background, what we're about, you know, our whole story."

Disastrously, June sat on the edge of Dawn's desk and settled in.

"Of course!" Dawn managed to say cheerfully.

"We've been operating for nine years this spring. I've been the executive director for seven of those nine years." A clear note of pride rang in June's voice, a verbal puffing of her chest. She seemed to be winding up for a long, beloved story.

"And we have always had at our core, as our core value, the idea of love. Love for art and love for empowering youth. Our mission has always been to express that love, to translate that love through exceptional programming.

That's what I've come to realize our mission really is—giving back with love. Teaching with love. We really make a difference in these kids' lives, you know, Dawn. We really do. You can see the effects, the effects in them when they return for more and more classes, and they have more and more confidence in themselves. More trust in us. It's quite hard for a lot of these kids to trust, you know? To trust any kind of authority figure. Some of them have been so badly abused. But what we do, it really makes a difference. Really helps them out. So we knew that what we were doing was the work of love. We always knew that."

June spoke quickly, gesturing with her hands, gearing up to some grand reveal.

"So we looked for a way, for a belief system, to operate the organization by prioritizing love. We specifically asked the consultant for this in our strategic planning session—this was three years ago now. And so, we decided we would adopt the tradition of the most ancient people of the earth. The most ancient and—I'll say it—the wisest! Once you understand a bit more about the culture and the teachings, you really start to see how central love is to everything in the ancient traditions. And quite a few of the kids who come here are Aboriginal, so it was a perfect fit!"

At this point, June smiled knowingly at Dawn, whose throat went dry.

"We operate by the Seven Grandfather Teachings here, Dawn. I'll give you the pamphlet about it. One of those teachings, one of those core values, is love. We operate with love here. And we think you'll be able to relate to the kids here really, really well. We really do. We're so excited to have you."

June rose from her spot on Dawn's desk and smiled down at her benevolently, placed a hand briefly on her shoulder. Dawn flinched away from June's touch and smiled in an attempt to mask it.

"Thanks for, uh, sharing that with me. It was ... inspiring."

June regarded her for what felt like a lifetime, and then smiled. "Operate with love, Dawn. Always remember that."

Then June turned and walked the five steps to her own desk, sank into her chair, turned to her computer screen, and began clicking resolutely away, staring straight ahead.

All the things that Dawn did not have the words to say, the weight of silence generations deep, felt heavy enough to sink her low, to bury her in the ground.

CHAPTER NINE

Martin's garage is cold but bearable, and it quickly becomes their hangout spot because they can smoke there. Cody tosses a beer to Dawn, then Crystal, then Tyler, droplets of cold water arcing across the cement floor behind every can. Lastly, Cody cracks one for himself. They sit in a rough circle in camping chairs, the old radio on the back shelf always tuned to the Oldies station, even though Dawn hates it, a space heater in the corner sizzling red, puffing warm air that quickly dissipates into the chill of the evening. They wear toques and boots and thick socks, a couple of sweaters and good jackets. The beer helps keep them warm, too. Tyler and Cody both smoke constantly, rapidly filling the Folgers' can at their feet with butts.

This is what passes for my social life now, Dawn thinks ruefully, glancing around at this unlikely crew.

Crystal's parka is short, puffy, and white, with a brown faux-fur collar. Her toque is a chunky pink knit with a floppy pompom that bobs and weaves when she moves. She drinks beer at a brisk pace and smokes far more weed than Dawn would have ever expected. She always leaves at nine thirty to drive the few minutes home and say goodnight to her kids. She's been around more and more lately, and Dawn looks for the quick glances, the casual physical contact that spells out f-u-c-k-i-n-g. She hopes it's Tyler but suspects Cody.

Dawn snaps out of her musings to find Tyler looming over her chair. She cranes her neck to look up at him.

"Can I help you?" She tries for cool and collected but lands on irritated. *Oh, well.*

He grins. "Touchy, touchy. Just offerin' you some weed, princess." He holds a joint out to her, half crushed between his indelicate fingers.

She accepts the joint and nods in acknowledgement of her hostility. That's all she'll give him. She hasn't been able to place Tyler's slight drawl or pin down where exactly he's from yet. He avoids her questions artfully, his answers vague, meandering stories, full of tangents and leading to no point at all, but Dawn has been collecting clues and hints, peppered throughout his lengthy and frequent orations. He's probably from Alberta—he's definitely spent some time in Calgary and its surroundings, working for the oil rigs, that much she's gleaned. Dawn isn't sure how working the rigs led to teaching code to prisoners, though.

Here's what she does know: Tyler and her brother are spending a lot of time together somewhere. Somewhere that is not sanctioned by Cody's parole requirements, since he's essentially only allowed to be at home or job interviews.

Martin forwarded Dawn the email with Cody's parole documents attached, and she'd dutifully reviewed them, since they both knew Martin wouldn't. However, Jim, Cody's parole officer, hasn't been by to check up on him yet. The threat of random check-ins was meant to hang over Cody, but Jim missed their first appointment. He called Cody an hour and a half after the start time, saying he'd gotten the dates mixed up and could they reschedule?

Crystal is drunk, maybe very drunk. She's shed her toque and scarf and partially undone the zipper of her puffy parka.

"How are Jake and the boys?" Dawn asks, and Crystal takes a beat, barely a breath's-length too long, to reply.

"Jake and the boys are great—they're just … great." Everyone hears the weak way her sentence fizzles out, the strained cheerfulness in her voice.

There is definitely a crack there, thinks Dawn.

"Well, that's good," she says out loud.

There's a moment of awkward silence, and then Crystal turns to Tyler and asks, "Were you ever married?"

Dawn pretends to read the label on her beer but watches

Tyler out of the corner of her eye. It's a pretty half-assed attempt at concealing her curiosity, so she just turns and looks at him full on, waiting for his answer.

Tyler smiles at Crystal like he's glad she asked the question. "I was," he says with a sage little nod. "Quite a while ago now—no need for your pity." He holds his hands up playfully, palms out, as though to ward off an onslaught. Nobody says anything.

He clears his throat. "We got married...well, I guess when we were twenty-two years old. So yeah, I was married once. But it didn't last."

Crystal is bobbing her head compulsively to Tyler's story like she's agreeing with each statement. Cody is bent low, doubled over at the waist, fishing a beer out of the cooler beside him, his face stormy. Cody and Tyler have barely interacted this evening, and Dawn half-hopes they're getting sick of each other.

Dawn's distrust of Tyler grows the longer he hangs around. He's loud and overbearing, bombastic, but he cuts it with so much perfectly timed and delivered charm, infuses his speech and mannerisms and behaviours with such unexpected, chivalrous touches that one can start to overlook his lesser qualities. One can, but Dawn can't. She sees Tyler like a man in a suit—not a business suit but a mascot costume. Big and bulky, with no way for the person inside to see out, let alone for anyone outside to see who's in there. It could be anyone. He projects a certain man, creates the atmosphere of a certain man, around himself through his insistence, with words and actions, that he is that man. But Dawn knows he is not. She knows that he's really the man in the suit.

She tunes back into the conversation to hear Crystal talking, her voice pitched a shade too high and a touch too loud, about how hard it is to sign her boys up for leisure activities through the city. Cody is nodding like he can relate, commiserating like he's had the exact same trouble with the website. Dawn watches the familiar contours of Cody's face, the way it opens up unexpectedly when he smiles or laughs, offering a tantalizing glimpse of the vulnerable boy he once was. She watches him smiling now. It doesn't reach his eyes.

Dawn wonders if they will ever talk about what happened, about what Cody did. She has no idea how to break this dome of silence over them. She's afraid of what she might ask him, and of what his answers might be. She cannot fathom an answer that would bring any sort of satisfaction. She feels the whoosh of her blood pressure dropping, the beginning of pins and needles in her hands and feet, at the mere thought of opening her mouth to ask: *Why?*

This should be a happy homecoming, but Dawn can't relax. She has no idea how to enjoy her brother's company. She can feel a great rending scream starting in the pit of her, a scream that will surely rip not only her but the world in two. She'd release it, but she knows it would only be met with mute stares or averted eyes. She'd release it, but it would only echo around the cold garage.

Crystal leans toward Cody to show him a video on her

phone. It stops and stutters, loading at a glacial pace with the bad Wi-Fi connection. Dawn's throat dries out and her eyes prickle. She looks away from Crystal and Cody to see Tyler, leaning back in his lawn chair, legs crossed at the ankles, watching her. She pretends not to notice and quickly downs the rest of her beer.

"I think I'll call it a night," she says, standing up.

Crystal and Cody half wave at her, distracted by the phone, and Tyler watches her cross the garage and go inside. Dawn leans against the closed door for a moment, feeling the cold air pressing at her back. She imagines she can feel Tyler's gaze, too, and shudders.

She lies awake that night for the countless night in a row, watching the shadows on her ceiling and imagining they're relaying secret messages she can't decipher. She lies in bed and watches the shadows dance and mock her, watches one shadow over by the door in particular, one that may have the shape of a woman with long, long hair. A half-figure, barely there in the waning darkness. The soft moonlight flickers and shifts; a hand reaches out in the dark.

Dawn rolls over, turns her back on the machinations of the night, and closes her eyes. The long, undulating wail of a siren comes closer, closer, crescendoes to a shriek, and then fades away. She wonders, bleakly, what emergency it's racing toward.

DAWN AND CRYSTAL crouch beneath the tallest wooden tower of the well-below-code play structure at the park, the rigid plastic swell of the slide above their heads. The plastic gets so hot in the blazing summer sun that it turns tacky to the touch, and the metal bolts that fasten it in place get hot enough to burn exposed skin that's carelessly pressed against it.

Dawn is wearing a floral-print sundress, sewn by Violet, who could lose herself in the rhythms of the sewing machine for hours. Violet makes piles of dresses for Dawn, who rarely consents to wear them, but she's wearing one today because there was a stain on the pink dress from the mall that she'd wanted to wear. Crystal has grown over the summer, making her jean shorts pinch her thighs and her favourite pink T-shirt ride up. The girls are becoming aware of their bodies being observed— and judged—by others and it makes them feel so profoundly awkward and ashamed that it's like they're wearing their own skins wrong. It's a strange, distancing feeling that they don't talk about, couldn't possibly articulate, but they both feel it, the first stirrings of a discomfort that will persist, tracking them through adolescence and long into adulthood.

For the moment, they're huddled under the tower, trying to tie dandelions together. They watched Alice in Wonderland *in Crystal's basement the other day for the thousandth time and decided today to try recreating the flower crown Alice made for her kitten. Their hands are clammy and the stems of the plucked dandelions ooze a liquid that makes the weeds wet and limp and difficult to tie together.*

"I'm bored!" Dawn hurls the dejected-looking tangle of flowers to the ground.

Crystal looks hurt. "What do you want to do?"

"Go to the far park?"

Crystal's face pinches, but she relents quickly. "Fine. Let's go."

The far park is a five-minute walk away, a few streets over from their block but still firmly within the bounds of the neighbourhood. It's less a park than a half-hearted landscaping feature with a path running through it, but it has a certain charm because it also has a small manmade pond. The gravel path leads to the vaguely kidney-shaped pond that sits in the divot formed by gentle slopes ringed by wooden and chain-link backyard fences. There isn't much to do there but skip rocks across the surface of the pond, but it's a change of scenery. They're both too lazy to go for snacks and slushies at the convenience store that stands alone like a sentry in a small paved parking lot next to the highway at the entrance to their neighbourhood.

The pond is a sparkling, deep grey-blue, dotted with the fat ducks and mean geese every kid in the neighbourhood feeds stale bread. The surface glimmers in the sunlight. Only the murky reeds along the pond's outer edges hold on to the light instead of reflecting it.

As the girls make their way down the winding path to the water, the shadow of a cloud dampens the sparkle. It's hot, but there's a welcome breeze. They pick a spot at the edge of the pond where the reeds are less dense. There's no sand here—the thin shoreline is composed of pebbles and rocks, and, as always, large areas are covered with white and green gobs of goose shit. They find a relatively clean patch of rocks and started scanning for flat stones to skip.

Dawn sees a clean, round, flat one and crouches to grab it. As she does, the breeze comes across the pond, carrying the faintest hint of salt, and something else. It lifts the fine hairs on Dawn's arms, slides along her cheek, and pulls her gaze to the three pine trees on the far side of the pond. The three tall pines stand partway up the far slope of grass, forming a rough circle.

The green boughs flicker and crackle as they sway.

The air between the trees shimmers, like the pond.

There is a buzzing in the marrow of Dawn's bones and in her ears.

Is it calling to her?

She comes to standing waist-deep in cold water.

Crystal is shouting her name in a panic from the shore, help-lessly waving her arms above her head, moving forward to dip the toe of her sneaker into the water before backing away and calling out anxiously again. Her voice is ragged.

Dawn wades back to the shore, confused and freezing. Her shoes are soaked through. She stands, shivering and dripping, before her friend. Crystal's eyes are so wide they're perfectly round, and Dawn laughs. Crystal slaps her, quickly and with no real force. Shocked, Dawn is about to retaliate when she sees that the whole of Crystal's small body is quaking, a dark stain down the inner seam of her tight shorts.

"What were you doing?" Crystal's voice is a sob.

"Didn't you … hear that?"

Crystal shakes her head.

Dawn looks back over her shoulder—the trees are completely still.

THE NEXT MORNING, Dawn wakes early, yanked from a dream that is really a memory. Her thighs and back are slick with cold sweat, and she's bound herself tightly with her sheet. She kicks the tangled, damp sheet loose from her body and lies looking up at the ceiling, the dream-memory keeping her half-anchored in the world of sleep.

This memory stayed with Dawn, tucked away in a back cabinet of her mind. Now that it's been unlocked, she realizes how she's felt since her brother came back. Like she's just opened her eyes and is standing waist-deep in a frigid pond with no recollection of how she got there. Or maybe she's Crystal—terrified and calling out from the shore.

Dawn is off-centre and cannot seem to right herself, like she's been falling ever since leaving Toronto. She's flailing, but slowly—she can see everything pass her by as she windmills through the air, desperate to find solid ground that isn't there.

CHAPTER TEN

TORONTO

Dawn opened the office door and flicked on the fluorescent tube lights, throwing her bag onto the nearest chair. It spilled open, pads and a lipstick, headphones and loose change scattering onto the floor. She stared at the mess in utter defeat for a beat before sighing and bending down to pick everything up. It was going to be one of those nights.

A restlessness had gripped her, taken hold and begun its slow creep a while ago.

It was about a year into her job. One evening Dawn made vision boards with a group of teenagers, a companionable silence holding them all. She carefully cut a night-blooming orchid out of a *National Geographic*, tracing the flower's delicate lines with her clumsy scissors. A girl with curly, dark hair and a black hoodie pulled down over her wrists pasted a picture of a mountaintop wreathed in mist to her board. A boy who couldn't sit still flitted between their table and the kitchen, where he was making popcorn in the microwave. The buttery smell filled the air and the radio played Top Forty hits in the background and Dawn had hoped that she and these kids would really be able to conjure up these visions in the year ahead.

At first, she'd imagined she would tap into some deep reserve within herself at her new job and impart life-long wisdom to the troubled youth that came seeking not just art but mentorship. Six months in, she'd adjusted that expectation somewhat.

Tonight was the first session of one of their newest workshops and Dawn was overseeing it, which meant she showed the facilitator around, helped her set up and clean up, and then locked up the office at the end. The facilitator was an earnest woman named Maryanne with lank brown hair and watery eyes who, according to her homemade website, was a "youth-oriented mindfulness coach and wellness expert." She would be teaching coping skills in a series of weekly meetings.

The vague subject of her program, and the even more unsettling vagueness of her credentials, left the actual content up to guesswork, which left Dawn mildly curious and distinctly annoyed. Dawn "managed" the programming at the centre now, but she didn't choose the speakers or facilitators—June did. Indomitable June, who soldiered on as the executive director, with no end to her tenure in sight.

The programming followed June's whims and friendships more than any established curriculum. One of the first programs Dawn sat in on offered unsound advice about crystal healing and juice detoxes. The presenter was a friend of June's named Kay, an aging hippie type with a mass of blond-grey curls piled messily on her head and a rather severe face for someone who still wore striped leggings and patchwork tunics. Luckily, the kids didn't absorb any of it because they were very bored and mocked her viciously once she left. Dawn told them not to be mean and also to get out, she had to close up.

Maryanne was June's good friend of many years. Dawn's Facebook stalking had revealed that June and Maryanne co-owned a renovated all-season farmhouse outside the city. June's profile had a photo album called *Vacation House* dedicated to their families' joint adventures—a shot of June and Maryanne with glasses of red wine in hand, lounging in front of the fireplace; a lunch at one of the many nearby vineyard restaurants, gently rolling hills in the background; two of the teenage children asleep on either end of a huge sectional couch, mouths open (captioned, "Too cute! Kids are zonked.")

Dawn flopped into her chair and a sense of peace at her aloneness washed over her; the office was palatial compared to the stifling box of a condo.

The initial sheen of the new condo had worn off. The linoleum flooring made to look like wood was peeling up at the corners and away from the baseboards; there was flooding from the units above (and theirs flooded into the unit below); for some crazy-making reason all the door handles were crooked; and on and on. Although Frances spent a lot of time at the library working on his thesis and Dawn spent as much time as possible at work, their place was still undeniably too small for two people.

But they didn't bring it up. Both of them resigned and unwilling to be the one to take the lead on apartment hunting in a city with bidding wars for renters and listings snatched up hours after they were posted. The silence wrapped itself familiarly around them, even as Dawn knew it would not make anything better.

Ultimately, she remained silent because still buried deep within her was the belief that being with Frances gave her a worth she otherwise wouldn't have. She pretended she didn't hate the way he cooked scrambled eggs, the way he cleared his throat in the morning. Pretended she still thought the sex was good, pretended she was fine with his emotional distance and his near-constant, gently delivered criticisms of her habits, her mannerisms, her choices. She pretended it was all enough for her.

More than enough—that she was *happy*.

What creeping shame it brought her to know, instinctively and unfalteringly, that she was not enough on her own. The shame crept and spread, and then it flared within her, everywhere at once. She was overtaken by it, consumed. That was all she was—shame.

And lately Dawn couldn't shake the wretched feeling

of dread that enveloped her, the feeling that her mother was desperately trying to reach her, to tell her something important. Her voice came with more frequency now, accelerating since the day in the elevator, though Dawn still couldn't piece together a message. Even still.

A warning, a warning, she kept thinking.

Sometimes she thought she saw the red and blue pulse of police lights on a wall or the sidewalk, but when she blinked, they were gone. She'd been having vivid dreams, where she watched her brother walk away down a long, long road.

She startled when her phone lit up and vibrated obnoxiously against the desk. Unknown number. It must be Maryanne, calling to be let into the building, which was locked by security after five thirty.

"Hello!" Dawn put a chipper note in her voice that rang hollow to her ears.

The voice that replied sounded like it was crossing a great distance to reach her.

"Dawn..." Her name was an accusation.

A tremor started in a deep pit within her. Dawn pictured an ill wind blowing across vast swaths of earth, homing in on her.

"Did you..." There was a noise obscuring the voice, not static but a kind of buzzing. The words came through disjointed. "See...did...see me...did see me?...See me? Did you? You? You see?"

Dawn hung up. She breathed so hard her throat felt rubbed raw.

His voice, stretched over seven long years, crying.

DAWN SAT AT a table near the back while Maryanne droned near the front of the room. About ten kids were spread out across four tables, and Maryanne was getting them to fill out worksheets to reveal their coping styles. Two of the boys were whispering loudly to each other, giggling, their sheets blank. Maryanne looked flustered as their voices rose. Dawn tapped her knuckles clear and loud on the table, and the boys turned to look at her. She gave them a look like, *Um, hello?* and they said, "Sorry," too loud and drawn out and turned back to their sheets, reluctantly picking up their pencils.

Dawn leaned back in her chair and wondered how she was going to sit through the whole workshop. She was nothing but a roiling sea, unable to find an anchor within herself. Frances was out tonight. He'd told her that morning while making scrambled eggs that he was meeting some colleagues from his PhD program to celebrate someone's research breakthrough. She'd nodded and smiled and said that would be a fun time, the information barely registering as relevant to her. She knew, when she was being honest with herself, that she didn't love Frances, didn't even particularly like him, as it turned out. Still, she slipped into her buried annoyance and regret each day and continued to smile at him across mugs of coffee in the morning, continued to allow him to roll over at night, place one hand on her breast, the other on her thigh.

Maryanne set up two chairs at the front now and got the kids to sit facing each other in pairs, practising some sort of coping exercise. Nausea seeped through Dawn's gut. Out of the corner of her eye, she saw a woman sitting at an empty table along the back row. Dawn squeezed her eyes shut, and when she opened them, the teens were getting ready to leave, pulling on jackets and checking the old-school bulletin board for new activity sign-up sheets. Maryanne was going table to table, gathering their discarded worksheets. Dawn must have fallen asleep, though it felt like she'd only shut her eyes for a few seconds. She stood shakily and walked over to Maryanne, certain her smile was an off-putting rictus.

"That was great," she said weakly, picking up some pencils from the table nearest her and looking around for somewhere to put them. There was no immediate solution in sight, so she pocketed them and then just stood there, unable to think of what she should be doing.

Maryanne deposited the worksheets neatly in the recycling bin by the office door. "Thank you. Do you think they enjoyed it? It's always hard to tell if you're getting through to them."

"Totally," Dawn answered absently, opening the office door so they could grab their bags.

"It was lovely to meet you," Maryanne offered as they parted ways on the sidewalk.

"Yeah, you, too. Thanks again."

It was still hot out, even though the sun was down, and Dawn was eager to get the walk over with and get home where she could blast the A/C. She had never been able to adjust to the humidity here.

The city stretched much farther out than Dawn's imagination could reach. There were whole areas she'd never been to. So many neighbourhoods she'd never know the energy and flow of, never know their hidden-gem cafés and diners and bakeries, the smoky corners of their dive bars. The thought of all that unknown life pained her sometimes—she imagined those areas across the city like warmly lit-up beacons in the night that she'd never reach.

She strode along a residential side street parallel to the busy main route lined with stores, wanting to avoid being around people in her current state. She passed homes with deep porches and two or three narrow stories, ranging along a spectrum of upkeep. Even the total gut-jobs cost over a million dollars; she couldn't estimate what was spent on the newly renovated ones. She walked by one ostentatious modern mansion overtaking three lots, all hard angles and strangely placed windows. As Dawn kept going west, the houses gave way to apartment buildings and scattered businesses. She came to a familiar sandy limestone building and realized this was the bar that Frances and his "colleagues" were at. It was an intimate, hipsterish place with layers of melted white candles in the front window, low lighting, and mismatched dark wood furniture. Frances loved it, claimed they had the best play-lists in the West End. She went with him occasionally and sipped tepid whisky ginger ales that always carried a hint of the other pop coursing through the taps, not really contributing to whatever conversation he and his friends were having.

As she approached the bar, she decided to go in and surprise him. The decision gave her an immediate and unexpected sense of relief. Gripped by a fear she couldn't articulate, she found that she wanted to see Frances right now. She wanted him to slip his arm around her, pull her toward him, kiss her on the side of her head. She was pleased to discover she wasn't quite as over the relationship as she'd thought. There was something to salvage after all. She'd work on it, work on herself. *It was worth it, wasn't it?* She couldn't expect a long-term relationship to always be easy; of course they'd have their ups and downs, times when they felt annoyed by the other person. You couldn't look anywhere online without seeing someone posting about how hard their relationship was, but that they wouldn't give it up for anything, because nothing worth having is easy. She was naive to think there wouldn't be lulls, wouldn't be times where she felt a suffocating stagnancy. She just had to commit herself to working through it.

She was sweating from the walk and the bar wasn't much cooler than outside when she pushed open the front door, the air heavy and damp with people and trapped heat. The ceiling fans whirred uselessly, defeated. She saw Frances and his friends almost immediately. Frances had on the blue-and-grey plaid shirt he'd been wearing earlier. It took her a beat to realize that his right arm was stretched out and around a woman beside him. His hand was stroking her upper arm in a gesture so deeply familiar that Dawn was momentarily frozen. The woman had shortish brown hair and was wearing oversized denim overalls on top of a small, tight white T-shirt. She threw her head back, and her laugh floated over to Dawn. And as she tipped her delicate head to the side and rested it on Frances's shoulder, Dawn saw who it was.

Gracie.

Gracie putting a hand to Frances's chest and rubbing it affectionately. Gracie laughing with all of Frances's friends, easily and brightly, lifting her drink in a mock toast. They all looked so comfortable with each other.

Dawn's blood slowed to stone. She turned and left before she could be spotted by the happy party. Her mind wiped clean and blank.

SUDDENLY SHE WAS HOME, pacing agitatedly in the narrow space between the kitchen counters and the couch. She couldn't seem to grab hold of her thoughts. She didn't know how much time had passed. She was shot through with anger and shame, with feeling so, so stupid, and a horrible, buzzing energy.

Her head whipped around like a hound catching a scent— the key in the front door. Dawn froze, her hands dangling limply at her sides. She heard Frances remove his shoes and walk down the hall. He stopped when he saw her.

He was half-cut, a sway to his lanky frame as he squinted at her uncertainly. She often came back to how he looked in this moment, just before: Frances, frozen in amber in his drunken state, head thrown back an inch too far as he studied her, cheeks flushed. Whatever he saw registered across his face as a twitch, an involuntary jerk of repulsion. That brief expression of disgust was passed down through fifty generations. Countless eyes stared at her.

Something rose inside her, and she didn't stamp it down.

It happened in an instant. It happened before she knew what she was doing.

Dawn stepped up to Frances and pulled the pencils from the workshop from her pocket. In a smooth movement, she plunged the pencils, three of them, into the meat of the back of his hand. They were sharp. One hit at an angle and broke, glanced off his hand, but the other two went in surprisingly deep. Frances didn't scream. He clutched his hand to his chest and looked at it with a waxen, blank expression, then at Dawn. Droplets of red blood welled up around the yellow pencils and flowed down his wrist. He pushed her with his other arm, a rough shove toward the door. She stumbled and then jogged to the door.

It was only after she was standing, dazed, in the lobby that she realized neither of them had spoken a word. Somehow, she had her purse and gym bag packed with some clothes and toiletries with her. *When did I grab these?*

A wave of nausea clutched her, and she clenched her teeth and stared fixedly at a point on the ground in front of her. In her periphery, she saw movement. A rivulet of blood coursed across the lobby floor toward her, snaking out from the mailroom around the corner. She looked away.

She was teetering on the edge of being here, in the fluorescent-lit condo lobby, and being in that alleyway in the inky winter gloom. The first drops of blood welled up a rich burgundy, then fell ruby red, apple red, down a wrist. She saw the smooth movement of a hand, again and again. An arc. And impossibly red blood, like paint splashed on the snow, up close, below her feet. She pressed the palms of her hands hard into her eyes.

Fresh air should help.

The night was cold, crisp, and still. Dawn needed to figure out where she was going to stay, tonight and longer term, and she needed her car, which was parked in the condo's underground parking lot. She realized that she should leave—she had no idea if Frances would press charges or … come looking for her or something, though that possibility seemed very out of character. She needed to leave. And then the second realization—the only place she could conceivably go was home. She still had a little money from her last paycheque, but it wouldn't last long. She had to go home.

She wondered how long Frances and Gracie had been fucking behind her back. Months? Years? In spite of her lukewarm feelings toward Frances, jealousy flared bright and hot. Alongside the intense flare of jealousy was the deepening sensation of being incredibly stupid. She felt like a class-A fool, and being the cause of this feeling was Frances's real unforgivable sin. That feeling made Dawn wish she'd aimed higher with the damned pencils.

On her way to the parking garage, she called work

and left a message on her and June's shared answering machine, knowing her words were probably thick and heavy and not caring. By the time June listened to it in the morning, Dawn would have the centre's number blocked in her phone.

She wished she could say goodbye to the kids, the ones who showed up regularly and whose lives and passions and wants and needs she felt she knew. She would miss them.

She wrapped herself in the big camping sleeping bag she always kept in her trunk for lack of storage and slept in her car. She leaned the passenger seat all the way back and curled into herself tightly in the chilly night, dreaming that Frances was yanking open the car door every time she fell asleep and jerking awake to stare panicked into the empty parking garage.

At four thirty a.m. she gave up on sleep and started the car. She set off, glancing only once at the condo building as it disappeared in the rear-view. Driving through the still-dark, nearly empty streets, she cruised quickly to the edge of the city. As the sun started to crest the horizon, she heard Violet's voice in the static of the radio while she was searching for a station. She kept searching. There were too many things pressing up against her now, pushing at her back. She sped down the highway toward the place she'd been avoiding for these long years.

CHAPTER ELEVEN

Although it's barely ten p.m. the house is quiet and dark. Martin goes to bed early. He's finally moved out of the dank basement and back into the main bedroom. The air outside is starting to turn toward the harsh bite of winter, the crispness of fall giving way to pure cold, especially at night.

Dawn's in her room, watching TV on her small laptop. On the drive back home from Toronto, she'd worried that Frances would call the police on her. She'd spent hours alternating between peering anxiously in the rear-view mirror, half-believing she'd see a cadre of police cars, sirens blaring, suddenly appear in the distance, and reassuring herself that, even if he had called the cops, they don't typically mount nationwide searches for pencil assaults. She wants to laugh now at the memory, but she thinks the laugh would maybe be the half-crazed kind, verging on tears.

She has an unread Facebook message from Casey that she's assiduously avoided looking at for months. The only message she's gotten from anyone from her life there. It begins, *Holy shit man, wh*—and that's all Dawn can see without clicking the message and showing she's read it.

She knows she'll never read it, yet she doesn't delete it.

She lies sideways in bed and doesn't bother to adjust the screen, watches the actors move at an angle, heads tilted like dog's listening for a whistle. Dawn hears a noise in the living room. The sound is lost as soon as she hears it.

She swings up and out of bed and crosses the room in a few strides. As she steps into the dark hall that leads to the bathroom, she hears someone clear their throat from the direction of the living room. She moves slowly down the hall and three figures come into view, backlit by the bright moonlight coming from the front window. Even in silhouette, she knows immediately that one is Cody and one is Tyler. The third is a short, muscular man she doesn't recognize. The short man's arms are crossed and agitation steams off him in waves. He's gesturing at the window—no, he's gesturing downwards, toward their feet.

In the deeply shadowed dark, the floor there has a different quality.

Dawn conceals herself just inside the open bathroom door, peering around the frame. As she stares at the spot on the floor, she registers a faint hissing, like a kettle beginning to build up steam. The short man is gesturing, emphatically, at the floor. Tyler and Cody are standing on either side of him with their arms crossed and chins tucked in, nodding and looking placidly at the place his hands indicate.

Oh Christ. She jerks her head back, realizes she's gripping the wooden door frame painfully with her fingers.

The floor moved.

She's certain she saw a ripple of movement. Her stomach is icy cold and turbulent.

The kettle is shrieking now. Boiling water hitting flesh. There's a chemical scent in the air like electricity, maybe a hint of salt, something Dawn can't name.

The stranger seems to be imploring Tyler and Cody, who are unmoved, pleading with them. As the man turns to Cody, her brother meets his eye, shrugs, and kneels down. He crouches at the edge of what Dawn can now see is a hole of deepest black. It appears to hover over the floor. The hole is not in the floor; it's in the air, the atmosphere, just above it.

Seeing this, Dawn has the sensation of a break occurring somewhere inside of her. A seismic break at the core of herself. She cannot take in what she's seeing because it holds only one meaning: *impossible.*

Cody kneels at the edge of the hole in the air and gazes into it, an act that seems to agitate the stranger further. He says, "Get up!" loud enough for Dawn to hear. Tyler lets his arms drop to his sides, his body slackening but with an undercurrent of tense energy. Cody remains static on the floor, at the edge of the hole, looking into it. The hiss subsides.

Cody is now moving his head ever so slightly and squinting his eyes—he's listening to something.

Dawn strains to hear, but then suddenly she doesn't need to strain anymore. There's a buzzing, like the sound of an immense electric grid or a great machine whirring to life. Deep in the layers of noise there's a certain tone, or rhythm maybe, that suggests a vocalization. It's coming from a very distant place, and it's resonating in the marrow of her bones, a buzz, a pull, and just as she thinks she can distinguish a new sound rising, everything ends. There's a sudden and complete silence that seems to scream in her ears. She feels dazed, disoriented.

The men in the living room step backwards, and she looks down and sees that the hole is gone. They gesture in frustration. She steps, too, retreating quietly down the hallway until she feels her bedroom door at her back, then slips inside.

She's trembling as she climbs back into bed.

THE NEXT MORNING, Dawn pushes a cart with a squeaky wheel up the shampoo aisle of Shoppers Drug Mart. Sometimes she come to walk the aisles even when she doesn't need anything, soothed by the neatly laid out rows of toiletries and medicines. She stops and looks at the packaging on all the hair products, comforted by the pinks and purples, blues and greens, the sleek lines, the lettering arranged to please the eye. Sometimes she leaves the packaging on things she buys for days, weeks even, because she can't bear to break the spell, the unfulfilled promise. The satisfaction she can feel from looking at beautifully packaged items is deep and pure. It's not about whether the product is good or bad, works well or not. It's about how good it looks, perfectly packaged. It's about the symmetry of something doing exactly what it's meant to do—it's meant to look good, and it looks good.

She's here to get frozen hash browns for breakfast, but she also needs to buy herself some time outside the house. She woke up with the insurmountable feeling that something had shifted, and she is afraid. She wants to slip away from her mind, away from what she saw last night. But she can't control where her mind takes her.

Dawn is always being pulled back, pulled back to that cold night in the lane.

Always, she comes circling back to the police arriving, to the knife lying on the frozen ground, to the boy lying on the frozen ground.

Both now, irrevocably, inert objects.

DAWN SITS IN A SMALL, *chilly interview room, across a rectangular table from two cops. She is not under arrest. They've said this to her several times already. Dawn is cold, and the damp, unwelcoming room isn't helping. The carpet in the small waiting area is thin and brown, reminiscent of a doormat. The computers are clearly old, and a big, clunky printer lurks behind the woman at the front desk. A worn-looking water cooler stands against one wall, tiny diamond-shaped paper cups teetering in a pile on top. The kind you have to refill fifteen times to get anywhere near quenching your thirst. The fluorescent strip lighting flickers half-heartedly. Dawn and the officers look sallow and wan underneath it, sitting unevenly around the table.*

"I guess I came around the corner the same time as the police?…The headlights were right in my eyes…"

Dawn's voice is flat and dull, except when it wavers uncertainly upwards. She feels disjointed and outside herself, like she's watching the action from a distance. Something huge threatens to make itself known from behind her ribs, presses urgently against her. Her lips, the tips of her fingers, tingle. She feels split in two. Tunes in and out of their questions.

The officers take notes, even though there's a recorder on the table between them, its red eye holding Dawn in its gaze. They nod along to her words. They are brisk and efficient, barely making eye contact with her, in a hurry to be somewhere else.

She tunes back in to the dull drawl of one of the officers. "Did your brother know the victim?"

Dawn blinks. "Yeah, I guess, kind of. We kind of know him."

"Was there any bad blood between your brother and the victim? Did they ever fight before?"

"No." Dawn shakes her head. "No, not that I ever saw or heard of." She floats away and hears herself saying, "He just hung around. He was always around, but we didn't really know him. Kind of weird?" She watches the officers scribble on their notepads.

"Loner. Violent?"

There's a buzzing in the room, or a grinding of metal, inten-
sifying. She looks up at the fluorescent lights. There's an urgency
to the buzzing that implies a will, a motivation. A need.

"Can you hear that?" she asks.

The officers shake their heads together, like two choreographed
spaniels.

WHEN SHE GETS HOME, Dawn watches her hands shake
as she dumps crispy hash browns, bordering on burnt,
onto a large plate.

Cody is caught up in something that can only bring hurt.

She thought there'd be time once her brother was out of
prison. Time to become close again, time to find the words
to talk about what he did. She can't believe she'd been
so glaringly stupid, but she realizes now that she'd still
pictured Cody as the twenty-year-old he'd been when he
went away. But Cody—*obviously*, she admonishes herself—
had not sat unchanging in prison. He'd aged, and changed,
as the years passed.

Dawn has no idea what prison was like for Cody.
Probably cannot know. Another divide.

Dawn is startled from her thoughts by her father's hand
on her shoulder. She brushes it off instinctively, without
thinking. Turns just in time to see the wounded look on his
face, replaced by a bleary smile. "Morning. You're making
breakfast?"

Martin pulls a mug from the cupboard, which has
remained neat and organized since Dawn attacked the

foul kitchen. He pours coffee and settles into one of the wooden chairs, peers at her in that irritatingly benevolent way he has, or maybe affects sometimes, like he has wisdom to impart. She can feel him lurking behind her, wanting to say something, waiting for the right moment. This puts her on edge, as it always has.

Every once in a while, when Dawn and Cody were younger, he would try, for an evening or two, to be the kind of father who talked to his children about their lives, who listened and doled out advice, but it never got very far because he was not that kind of father. They didn't have that kind of relationship, and Dawn wasn't sure he was entirely to blame for that, but it didn't make it untrue, and it didn't make her anger go away. She thought they should have that kind of relationship, and the distance between them gnawed at her more for this reason than for the fact itself.

Dawn rinses the dregs of the coffee in the sink and starts a new pot brewing. Tries to make brisk, efficient movements, to seem busy and purposeful, distracted. She's not distracted; she's laser-focused on her annoying-ass father, still silently staring at her back. Whatever he has to tell her, it won't be welcome.

As far as his kids know, Martin, like Violet, is without a past. He never speaks about his family, just like Violet never spoke about hers after they stopped seeing them. When Dawn and Cody were little, Martin would deflect all questions about his parents, about whether he had siblings, by putting on a goofy smile and saying they'd all packed up and moved to Timbuktu. They have never met any of Martin's relatives. Violet's relatives were around, sometimes—until suddenly they were not. Dawn has memories of visiting someone else's house across the city, with a rec room full of raucous aunties and uncles and a TV playing hockey, and her mother's hands fluttering nervously over a casserole dish in the kitchen, and cousins running amok, weaving among the adults' legs, her mother looking down at the floor.

But that stopped. Something changed, or solidified, in Violet, and they stopped going to that house, and no one ever came over to theirs. When they asked Violet where she grew up, she would only reply "The bush," with a slight wistful or rueful smile on her face, but she never elaborated, and after they stopped seeing her family, Dawn and Cody stopped asking. They lived in silence instead.

As a teenager, Dawn spent hours daydreaming away the dampening quiet of their home. She imagined her family was one that existed in a bubble of sound—happy laughter and glasses clinking in a jovial way, not a lonely way, and relatives' voices overlapping. She imagined a life full of the joy of other people. She felt a shapeless sort of grief that she couldn't name. She was a person with her context written on her face, written on her body, but it was unknown to her. When kids at school or Crystal mentioned their grandparents, she couldn't conjure up any memories of her own.

There is some heavy and dark wood furniture in the living room that they knew had come from Martin's parents' place, and Violet had a plain silver bracelet of her mother's that she kept in her bedside drawer, but that was it. The extent of the family history they had. Dawn thinks it was this shared refusal of the past that brought her parents together. Making her and Cody the products of a relationship built on the ability to turn permanently away.

Both her parents were islands, leaving Dawn with a deep cavern inside, a formless space of loss whose depths she did not know. That empty space where other people should have been. Where *their* people should have been. She could not yet explore this particular void, but it was ever-present in the background of herself, and she knew that one day she would have to face it.

And she wondered, above all else, why her parents could only give their children this fractured kind of love.

"What is it, Dad?" she says finally, a bit more peevishly than she'd meant to. She turns to face him, leaning against the counter and holding her mug of coffee protectively in front of her. *I am casual*, she recites to herself. *I control my emotions.*

"Just … how are things going? I know it must be a big adjustment, comin' back here, and your brother comin' home …"

"It's good. I'm good, Dad." *Is that it?*

"Were you … um. Were you planning on staying … a long time? Not that you're not welcome! You are. Always. Just, like, are you gonna get a job or something? Don't you think you need something to do during the day?"

He's spoken these last few lines very fast, and then taken

a sip of coffee, avoiding making eye contact with her. Dawn is momentarily stunned, before the embarrassment flushes through her system. Her dad's telling her to get a job? Like she's some freeloader? True, she isn't paying rent, but he hasn't asked. And she's been contributing to groceries.

She narrows her eyes at him. "Is Cody telling you to kick me out?"

"What? No! Why would…why would Cody be telling me that? Honey, you just seem a bit…down-and-out. I think you need something to do during the day, that's all."

Last night has left a residue of dread and nausea, and she knows this is contributing to how intensely irritated she feels right now. Her dad, the man who was living like a troll in the basement when she arrived, thinks she needs to switch up her lifestyle? *I'm recovering*, she wants to tell him. Refuses the thought of *lying low*.

The future before her is a great, gaping expanse of nothingness. She feels the weight of failure pressing steadily downward, amorphous and so crushing in its completeness that it leaves room for nothing else.

Dawn bites her lip. "I'm trying," she says. And then it's too much, and she walks out of the kitchen.

CHAPTER TWELVE

I t's a bleary, grey afternoon a few days from Halloween and Dawn hasn't been able to fully wake up. She feels muted, like the sky, though an ever-increasing undercurrent of anxiety runs through her, ever since the night she saw ... whatever it was that she saw. Was she dreaming? She can't make sense of it, of the feeling like electricity dancing, prickling over her skin, of a chasm in the air.

On her way to her bedroom for a nap, fatigue heavy in her joints and behind her eyes, she pauses outside Cody's closed bedroom door. She imagines she can feel him there, and she thinks about knocking. She can't know that he is just on the other side of the door, his sweaty back pressed up against it as he shakes, tremors running through his whole body, like he's shivering in an Arctic cold. He's clenching his jaw so tightly that his molars grind sickeningly off each other. Cody is coming apart. Or he's already fallen apart. He's in a million pieces, floating out of reach. He is just parts, no whole.

She doesn't know this, and she doesn't knock.

She climbs into bed fully clothed and is asleep quickly.

SHE'S SITTING ON the front step of their house, Cody sitting next to her. They are both looking straight ahead and their knees are almost touching. There's the sense that someone is standing behind them, but Dawn's neck is heavy and she can't turn to look. Cody is talking, and she catches the last of his words "... You weren't supposed to be here."

"Cody, who is Tyler? What's going on?" she asks, and she wants to turn and look at her brother, but she still can't move her head.

And then Cody is talking like a radio broadcast tuned in partway through, a steady, monotone stream:

"... started coming to my cell at night. I thought I was losing my mind for real, seeing ghosts. Being in there will make you think you're losing your mind, you know? But he started coming every night, and he'd just stand in the corner, not saying nothing, and Brandon, my cellmate, he didn't see him.

"Then one night he came over and sat on the edge of my bed, of the cot. And he started talking to me. I thought the guards were gonna come any minute, I thought Brandon was gonna wake up, but nothing happened.

"And the shit he told me, Dawn, was unbelievable. Couldn't understand all of it, but it was unbelievable. He talked about some plan.

"He buzzed, he kind of vibrated. He talked about portals. I could see his eyes somehow, even in the dark. And I listened. I really listened. I didn't know what he wanted me to do, but I knew I was in. He said he'd get me out, he'd take care of things."

Dawn senses the presence behind them is agitated, angry, she can't turn to look, but she feels a rage, a hate, directed at her back, and it feels like the distance is growing between her and Cody, like the front steps are widening, like she's floating off alone somewhere. She calls out to her brother.

"How did it feel, Cody?"

And as she goes, as she's wrenched away, she hears Cody's answer as though across a great void.

"It felt like nothing at all."

DAWN WAKES WITH her mouth dry and the sheets tangled. The dream is gone. She drifts out to the living room. The house is empty. She stands for a minute looking out at the street and watches a white garbage bag ghost hanging from a tree twist in the wind.

IT'S HALLOWEEN NIGHT. Dawn, Cody, Crystal, and Tyler are sitting in the garage, bundled up, with the door open. The mini candy bars for the trick-or-treaters are in a giant metal bowl set next to some poorly carved jack-o'-lanterns at the top of the driveway. They call out "Happy Halloween!" to each group of kids who shout "Trick or treat!" in sloppy chorus and dip their hands into the bowl, scooping candy into pillowcases, plastic bags, home-sewn totes decorated with ghosts and pumpkins.

Martin comes out to stand behind their semicircle of chairs, wearing a pair of worn moccasins that belonged to Violet—he rarely wears them so they don't fall apart, but he puts them on when he's in a particularly good mood. He sips his mug of peppermint tea. Dawn wants to say something positive about it, but she doesn't. Martin clinks the mug lightly against the back of Cody's head. Cody smiles and dips his head.

"Well, kids," he says after a short pause, "I'd better get back inside."

He leaves and Dawn stares for a moment at the space where he was. He is clearly much happier now that Cody is out, and he's really cut back on the drinking, yet she can't help but wonder how much of this happiness is a result of wilful ignorance on Martin's part. A refusal to see that something is wrong here. He doesn't ask Cody about Tyler. She wants her dad to take control of the situation, but he doesn't see, or pretends he doesn't see, that there even is a situation.

Dawn always has a stomach ache or a headache now, pounding away in the background, and her bottom lip is chewed ragged, gross and bleeding. She pops Advil with her coffee in the morning, again at dinner time, as they drink at night. She might be slowly rotting from the inside out. Dawn keeps telling herself the perfect moment to talk to Cody will arise, and she'll know it when it does. She's convinced herself of this. She can't face the real reason she can't, or won't, ask him what's going on, what he's got himself involved with.

She's afraid of her brother.

Cody is a stranger with her brother's face. She understands on some level that they became estranged that night, that moment. That there's a one-way abyss between them now, a chasm neither of them can ever cross back over. Surely what he did leaves some sort of mark on a person. She wonders how he can think of anything else. She wonders if he replays those seconds constantly, incessantly and automatically, like she does. Does the memory run through the back of his mind, like it does hers, colouring all his days? Does he dream about it at night, like she does?

Would Cody have talked to her if she'd visited him? Maybe that was her opportunity to ask him, to understand. Maybe she squandered her chance by not knowing what to say to him. Really, by not knowing how to face him. And now she fears that she doesn't know him anymore.

A man in dark Wrangler jeans and a leather bomber jacket trails two small figures in Teenage Mutant Ninja Turtle costumes up the driveway. Crystal runs toward them, clapping her hands.

"My boys!" she says in a funny accent, some inside joke that makes them giggle and fall against each other. "Did you get to lots of houses? How much candy d'you got? Enough for me?"

"Nooooo!" they cry in unison, clutching their precious booty to their tiny, concave chests.

Crystal kneels in front of the Ninja Turtles, straightens their wayward masks, hugs them to her. Jake has taken them trick-or-treating this year ("for the first time ever!" she'd crowed to them), so Crystal had gotten them dressed and sent them off, agreeing to meet up here after they (or, more likely, Jake) had their fill.

Jake straightens like he's gathering himself and steps into the garage. Dawn is sure his eyes flick to the bottle of beer on the ground next to Crystal's empty chair.

"Hi folks." He grins at them, smooth and calm. Raises a hand in greeting. "I guess we haven't all met before. I'm Jake Reed, Crystal's husband. You must be Dawn's brother." His eyes rest on Cody.

Jake and Cody would not have gotten along in high school. Jake would have been the kind of self-assured jock at the top of the high school pecking order. Cody floated outside the traditional hierarchies. There, but removed. Disliked—often intensely, by other boys—Cody had a certain bad-boy magnetism and boyish good looks that attracted girls from across the high school social order. Looking back, though, Dawn could see there'd always been an edge to his charm. Faint, and then more pronounced after he graduated high school, when the joking and the easiness could flip at any moment.

Cody jumps out of his camping chair, claps a startled Jake on the shoulder, and says, "Jake, man! Great to meet you, great to meet you. Jake Reed? Reed...Reed...You ever play Triple A?"

As they chat somewhat awkwardly, Dawn glances over at Tyler, who is staring fixedly at Jake's profile from where he's sitting about ten feet back in the garage. Dawn imagines Jake can sense the other man's stare. Jake doesn't look over but claps Cody on the shoulder in turn, and then slings an arm around Crystal and rubs her shoulder. He smiles at Dawn, waves, then nods to Tyler, who is smiling and nodding by the time Jake turns to him, the shadow of some darker emotion fleeing from his face.

Jake and Crystal head off down the driveway with the kids running ahead to a house with an elaborate scene out front: ghosts in trees, tilting tombstones, skeletons, a scarecrow on the porch, and some spooky Halloween-sounds playlist on a loop emanating from the open front door. Dawn watches the family walk away and wonders if Jake's grip isn't a bit tight on Crystal's arm.

When she turns back into the garage Tyler and Cody are talking in low voices, their heads tilted close together. Tyler grabs Cody's knee and shakes it twice, hard. He whispers urgently in Cody's ear as Dawn approaches. Cody glances up at her and pushes Tyler away, trying to cover the moment with a smile.

"Going out tonight?" she asks casually and is surprised when Tyler rejoins with, "Yeah, wanna come for a drink? Change of scenery wouldn't be bad."

And it happens again. Sometimes Tyler's voice goes peculiar as he speaks. Only ever for a few words at a time, his voice will go flat and mechanical. It's not a dramatic change, but it's there, it *happens*. Hollow and buzzing, like some giant, alien insect calling out from far away.

Dawn suddenly knows what it sounds like, the realization making her fingertips go cold.

It sounds like what came out of that black hole in the air. She shudders remembering the eerie buzzing, the energy, that had filled the living room that night.

"Okay," she says, thrown off, light-headed and too aware of the weight and bulk of her arms hanging at her sides. She crosses them over her chest, then uncrosses them. Breathes as deeply as she can.

Tyler smirks. "Leave in five?"

Cody is studying his nails, avoiding making eye contact with his sister.

"Okay," she says again.

She gathers her anxiety, her fear, and presses it down, down, as far as it will go. She needs to find out what the hell is happening here.

TYLER DRIVES A matte black BMW, not ostentatious but definitely not a car seen around South Saint Jude much. And definitely not on the labyrinthine downtown streets they are presently cruising. *How does a prison teacher afford this car?* Dawn wonders, as the neighbourhood rolls by.

Tyler's rough hands stroke the radio dial and the wheel like a lover, tender and careful. The analogy isn't right, though—Dawn doesn't think Tyler would treat a lover with such reverence. She stares hard for a few seconds at his profile from the back seat, and then looks back out the tinted window. She'd hoped, in some small part of herself, that Cody would take her to Al's as a nod to old times. But Cody doesn't speak about old times. For all she knows, he doesn't even think about them. Since the day he came home from prison and wept in the kitchen, he hasn't shown any more outbursts of genuine emotion.

The car creeps down a narrow residential road buried deep in the confusion of one-way and half-hidden streets that make up this part of the East End, a neighbourhood thickly layered in decades of municipal negligence, or outright hostility. They drive past a small but bursting community garden, tucked in a skinny vacant lot between two homes; an obvious trap house, a classic Tupac poster blocking out a second-floor window; tidily painted family homes with neat lawns; and big, ramshackle places converted into rooming houses, weeds choking the grass. The steely sky is smooth and uninterrupted like an over-turned bowl. The moon is bright enough to illuminate the curves of eaves, the blank flatness of windows reflecting the pale light and deflecting eyes like a spell of protection.

Just as Dawn is about to ask where the hell they're going, Tyler pulls up to the curb in front of a two-storey clap-board house and kills the engine.

Cody, silent the whole ride, opens his door and stands in front of the car, arms crossed over his prison-muscled chest, impatient. Before Dawn's even shut her door, Cody has started off around the side of the house, toward the back.

As Tyler and Dawn round the corner, Cody already has the screen door propped open and is knocking on the wood beneath. After a moment, there's a shuffling sound on the other side and the door opens to reveal a middle-aged woman, black hair tumbling wildly down past her shoulders and ruby-red lipstick smeared around her mouth. She has gorgeous brown eyes, even with eyeliner applied blotchily around them. She's wearing a navy-blue pencil skirt of some thick, unpleasant fabric, a blazer made of the same material, a white blouse with lipstick on the collar, and scrunched nude pantyhose. No shoes. A lit cigarette, cherry bobbing and weaving with the movement of her long fingers, trails from one hand.

"My darliiiiiiiing," she trills, as she reaches for Cody, patting him on the chest. "My big, bold darling. Come in out of the cold, love."

Cody grasps the hand that pats his chest and kisses it. "Mickey. Beautiful as always. Tyler's with me—and a friend. My sister, actually."

Dawn registers a flash of annoyance in Mickey's glassy, dark eyes, but she turns a sloppy yet bright smile toward Dawn anyway.

"Of course, of course." Mickey smiles and wobbles back from the door. "Come in, all of you, my loves. Come in."

The three troop over the threshold and shut the door behind them, which Tyler tells Dawn to lock. They leave their shoes on and walk through an empty kitchen, the air tinged with smoke and the faint scent of something else, something organic that's gone rotten. They head toward another door, which leads to the basement.

There's a built-in bar in the corner of the main room, and a small DJ booth in the far corner opposite. Aside from a patch of bare cement that serves as a dance floor, the ground is covered in overlapping woven rugs. Couches line the dark walls and a hallway leads off past the bar to a half-finished bathroom and another room, out of sight; Dawn can hear voices rising and falling, laughing. The air is thick with cigarette and weed smoke. About fifteen people are scattered throughout the main room and maybe as many more through the back.

A hand falls heavy on Dawn's shoulder.

She turns to see Tyler, who quickly hands her forty dollars before she can tell him off for startling her.

"They only take cash. Obviously," he says, then moves off toward the back room, following Cody.

Dawn decides she'll catch up with them after she gets a drink. Or two.

Having nowhere else to go, the smoke hangs thickly in the air and Dawn can already feel her lungs getting irritated. She'll pay for this tomorrow. But right now, she feels an undeniable thrill of excitement. She hasn't done anything like this in a long time, especially not with her brother. Maybe this will be a good night. Good enough to forget whatever the fuck is going on. Or to learn more.

The bartender is deep in conversation with a group of aging punks. Dawn listens patiently to their reminiscing for about ten minutes. This is not the kind of place to demand quicker service. Finally, after recalling and partially re-enacting an epic fight at a long-shuttered music venue, the bartender shoos away his buddies and nods toward Dawn.

Clutching two beers to her chest, she moves toward the back room. Tyler is slouched on a vintage-looking couch, low to the ground. For a second, Dawn thinks he's passed out, but he's only leaning awkwardly to the side, talking to a guy in an equally low brown chair. She sits down too hard next to Tyler, sloshing beer onto her shirt. He straightens up, stares at the stain on her tits, and smiles at her.

"Nice entrance. This is Paul." He gestures toward the guy in the chair.

"Hey, Paul. I'm Dawn." She toasts him with her beer bottle.

"Paul is ... a searcher. Much like myself." Tyler is still smiling. Dawn doesn't know what this means.

Paul looks at her levelly before nodding once and saying, "Hey, Dawn."

He settles back in his seat with no further attempt at conversation, looking off into the middle distance. They must both be on something, Dawn decides. She's mulling over how to create a conversation in this awkward vacuum when Tyler speaks.

"I dreamed about you, you know."

Dawn stares and feels a freeze move quickly through her body. This hated sensation that comes over her automatically, that has come over her since she was a preteen, when she doesn't know if a man is going to steer the conversation toward sex and she is, loathsomely, and only momentarily, afraid.

"What do you mean?" she says neutrally.

"In prison. The last few days before we got out. Cody had been telling me about you and Martin a lot. And I dreamt about you. Well, you're nothing like you were in my dreams! In my dreams, you were … sweet. Lovely."

Heat rises in Dawn's chest, her throat. *What the fuck?* She searches Tyler's face and sees that his pupils are huge and glassy. He seems to be looking through her. Paul has vanished from the brown chair.

"What did you say? What the fuck are you saying, Tyler?"

Her voice is rising noticeably. Everyone in the narrow room is turned toward them now. She's afraid her heart will burst with the strength of its beating.

"Before *we* got out?" she repeats. "You were in prison, too? Like, as a prisoner?"

"In a manner of speaking," he says slyly, and then a hand comes out of nowhere and clubs him on the ear, a sloppily thrown punch that still connects enough to get Tyler's attention.

Cody stands above him, furious, and as he goes to hit him again, Tyler grabs his wrist. They stare at each other for an uncomfortable beat, and Dawn is tempted to run, to sprint out of the room, up the stairs, and out. After a few tense seconds both men relax, the tension draining out of their stances. Tyler drops Cody's wrist.

"You're fucked up, man," Cody whines plaintively, motioning for Tyler to get up. He turns to Dawn. "Let's go. I just had to grab something off someone here."

Cody cuts his eyes at Tyler, who stumbles as he gets up and places a hand on Cody's shoulder to steady himself. Cody flinches, but rather than drop his hand, Tyler tightens his grip.

"Don't forget," Tyler slurs. A smirk curls his lips as he finishes his sentence: "Don't forget what you owe me."

Dawn can see that Tyler's made a bad mistake, and then Cody punches him square in the face.

They spill through the back door all at once as Mickey pushes them through it. Her lipstick is reapplied and she is keeping up a steady stream behind them: "… love you, man, but you can't fight in here! You know you can't fight in here, it's just the way it has to be, I don't really care if you slug the guy, do I? You just can't fight in here," and then she slams the door behind them, cutting off her words and the light from the house.

They stand outside bathed in awkward silence, broken by a dog in a nearby yard losing its mind. A deep, booming bark, like it's coming from a big dog, frantic at the end of a chain. The house has only one measly light directly above the back door, offering little illumination in the dark.

The drifted snow has deep pools of blackness beneath its crested peaks. Dawn thinks of the hole above the living room floor. Of Cody listening to something inside it. And there's something else beneath her fear, beneath the dread, something she's putting too much energy toward ignoring.

She's intrigued.

She can feel the wrongness woven through everything—and still, she wants to know. Some part of her wants to know, to understand—to ask if she can be a part of it, too. Why should Tyler, a virtual stranger to them, get to spend so much time with her brother? Share secrets with him, share some sort of bond? She can't think too much about this, though, or the most painful jealousy she's ever felt starts to constrict her throat.

There's a part of her that's drawn to the unseeable blackness beyond. And maybe that's why strange things have always found her. Maybe that's why Violet talks to her, why she can feel a buzzing sometimes, an insistent mechanical whine from somewhere distant that, if she listened hard enough, might turn out to be the sound of her name, hissing through a hundred thousand alien throats.

Shadows and light on the deep snow form rectangles of blue and black against the bright white. Some have crusty, dirty edges, re-frozen over where boots have previously broken through. Shards of ice shine on the tops of drifts like perfect, clear diamonds. An entire ecosystem of snow.

"Dawn!" Cody snaps at her, and she folds her arms defensively across her chest, unsure what she's missed. Tyler's face and upper lip are streaked with blood from his nose, which looks somewhat squashed, like it might be broken. He's breathing through his mouth, but there's a glint in his eyes, not of anger but, maybe, amusement?

"Sorry," she mutters, and Cody looks very annoyed, verging on outright angry, a tightness to his face.

"Why did you lie?" She blurts it out suddenly, maybe because Cody's already angry. "About Tyler being your teacher in prison?"

Cody looks at her, and although he's clearly fighting back annoyance, he says with forced nonchalance, "He didn't want to make a bad first impression."

Almost at the same time Tyler says, with a bizarre intensity, "I *was* his teacher."

Dawn takes a step back and stares at them both, but neither says anything more. It is freezing outside, the wind cutting straight through her jacket.

Cody exhales and stretches his arms above his head. "Look, let's just pretend we never came here, okay? Better for everyone."

Dawn doesn't want to argue anymore. Her teeth are chattering, and she presses her thighs together for any trace of warmth.

"I don't even know where we are," she mutters bitterly, and Cody shrugs and heads around the side of the house, back toward the car, agitation still roiling off his body.

Tyler's car heats up quick, unlike her beater. When she guesses they're roughly halfway home, she says, "So, what were you picking up there?"

She expects to be ignored, met with stony silence, but instead Cody reaches into his jacket, pulls out a manila envelope, and hands it to Dawn. She doesn't hesitate to upend it and shake out the single piece of paper inside. She can't read it. Handwritten in a scrawling hand:

Late night. Deep winter. Half-moon.

CHAPTER THIRTEEN

Each year the closest mall hosts a Santa Claus village, replete with a Santa for pictures, animatronic reindeer, fake snow galore, and incredible amounts of silver and gold glitter. It is a spectacle utterly out of sync with the semi-depressed mall around it. Still, it's erected each year, even as more stores close down and their storefronts remain empty. The display goes up in November and stays until New Year's Eve, though the option to take a picture with Santa is gone after the big day.

Dawn is momentarily stunned by it as she rounds the corner and it appears in the distance at the junction of several wings of the mall. It takes up the entire intersection that usually has couches and chairs set up as a resting place for weary spouses and children.

Facing Dawn as she approaches is a small hut labelled *Santa's Workshop*. An animatronic elf stands in the window, waving serenely, over and over again, a looping greeting into infinity. His face is a rictus, desperation in his plastic smile.

The workshop is made to look like a gingerbread house, and it is delightful. Its eaves are carved and curlicued, and sliver-glittered snow drips from the peaked roof like icing. The entire village is blanketed in a layer of fake snow, with drifts piling in soft mounds around reindeer and trees. Santa sits in the middle on a red-and-gold throne. A lord in his village, an emperor. A line of children and their parents' snakes out and winds around the side.

Dawn walks by a mother kneeling on the floor, imploring a red-faced, enraged toddler in a stroller to "Calm down for Mommy, Keenan! Calm down now!" in a nervous, high-pitched voice. Another mom is talking intently and non-stop into her phone tucked up against the side of her face as her child dangles off her other arm, yanking so hard Dawn worries the woman's shoulder will dislocate. A small boy holding a well-loved stuffed rabbit leans into his mother's leg and stares at Dawn without blinking, his eyes a shocking emerald green.

She moves away from the Christmas village. Dawn is not here for a picture with Santa. She's here to meet her brother.

When they were growing up, the mall was a haven, especially in winter. Somewhere they could hang out in a group without imposing so many kids on one set of parents, somewhere they were relatively safe, where they could spend a few hours indoors when it was frigid outside. Cody would slink off with some of the older boys, probably to smoke, and Dawn and Crystal would go touch the fur coats in the Bay with the other girls and Kyle, someone's little brother who always tagged along. She remembers him having an unruly mop of brown curls and being perpetually sticky. The saleswomen inevitably chased them from the furs, appalled.

Dawn sits down at a table in the food court, tossing her bag proprietarily on the seat beside her. The tables and chairs are those strange moulded mounds of plastic only ever found in mall food courts and university cafeterias, attached to each other in one thick, ungainly unit. These particular ones are brown and have not been updated for decades.

Dawn scans the crowd for Cody. It's been a few weeks since they went out together and Cody hasn't been home much; last night he surprised her as she was coming out of the bathroom, emerging from the dark of the hallway, his hands gripping her painfully on the arms, his voice a low, urgent whisper. "Tomorrow, meet me at the mall food court. Three p.m., okay? Please, Dawn." Then he walked quickly away. Seconds later, she heard the front door open and close. She'd slept fitfully, flowing in and out of fragmented dreams, odd images weaving together and then dissolving, reforming—bare black tree branches against a white sky; a snow-blanketed, rough field rolling away like the sea; something coarse-furred and big, shuddering; a glinting eye. Her brother holding out his hand.

It's a few minutes before three and Cody is not known for his punctuality. Dawn tells herself to calm down and be patient. But she ignores her own advice and scans the people in the food court relentlessly, like she's watching for a sighting of a rare animal on safari. Her impatience is, even to herself, a thin veil for her fear. And for that other thing. That tiny thrill of perhaps not quite excitement but of curiosity. She wants to know what the hell was opened up in their living room, what she hears calling to her. In her dream last night she also saw a black portal, swirling with unknown energy and buzzing, humming.

And under the terror and the curiosity, there is another fear—of rejection. She understands that Cody has chosen Tyler over her, yet she's afraid he'll say it out loud, he'll name it, which will make her feel the way she has felt too many times in her life. She's hijacked by an image of Frances in the bar, his arm draped around Gracie's petite shoulders. Tinkling laughter like salt in the wound floating toward her from their table. She hates herself for caring, for needing.

She's jerked from her memory when Cody sinks onto the chair across from her. She startles, and then recovers herself. A certain gravity hangs in the air. Something crucial is about to happen. A possibility cracked open when Cody asked to meet her here. Dawn can sense how delicate the moment is, like walking along the thinnest of tightropes.

"Hi, Cody," she says neutrally and looks at her brother head-on, really taking him in.

He looks like shit. He's losing the muscle he'd built in prison, and his cheeks are starting to look sunken. His skin is sallow and his lips are chapped. She feels like she's been here before. Then she has the unhappy realization that he resembles Violet when she was ill. The past settles onto the present, like time folded over onto itself.

"Hey, sis," he says, his voice flat, expressionless.

"Are you okay?" she blurts out without knowing she would.

He flinches, as though she's reached out and hit him.

"I..." he starts but trails off, distressed. He looks down at his clenched hands on the table.

Dawn doesn't move, hardly dares to breathe. The weight of the moment, wavering on some invisible cliff's edge within Cody, is nearly suffocating.

"I can't..." he starts and stops again, looking pained.

Then some resolve within him hardens, and he steps firmly back from the cliff's edge. He shakes his head quickly, then looks at Dawn with a new meanness in his eyes. When he speaks next his voice has venom in it.

"You need to leave town, Dawn. Why are you here, anyway? Kind of pathetic, isn't it?"

She stares at him, incredulous, too astonished to be angry or hurt. "Are you really calling me pathetic?"

She hardly recognizes her own voice. It is low and contemptuous, with a threatening undercurrent. Suddenly disgusted, with herself and with Cody, she snatches up her purse, preparing to leave. Then she pauses, and everything pours out.

"You're the one who's pathetic," she says, and she is crying as soon as she starts to speak. "You're a fucking loser, you're a…a…hanging out with that psycho, Tyler! I don't know what the fuck you've gotten yourself into, but it figures, doesn't it? It's fucking typical. You're the pathetic one, Cody."

She's sniffling back tears and snot and trying to get up out of the stupid, awful chair with as much dignity as she can. She's never said anything like this to her brother before, and something within her feels dangerously liquid, unmoored. Cody doesn't look shocked; he looks like he feels nothing.

But he says, "Wait," as she starts to walk away. And she doesn't, heart and blood pounding in her head.

She almost gets into an accident in the parking lot, driving half-blind with rage. She slams on the horn and screams inside the car, turning her angry face to sneer at the other driver—an elderly man hunched over and frail. Tears prickle the back of her eyes.

She *is* pathetic.

She parks in the driveway of her father's house and gazes at the drab winter colours.

She presses the palms of her hands hard into her eyes.

She goes inside.

Later, Dawn will look back on that winter, and her most vivid memories will be small fragments of the whole, sounds and glimpses. She will recall them in vibrant colour and exquisite detail—the rough texture of the jacket Cody wore, the bass tone of that strange, guttural noise Crystal made. The smell like an electrical fire, like the sea.

For a long time, she will remember only that Cody told her to leave, and she didn't. That he asked her to wait, and she didn't.

CHAPTER FOURTEEN

The world slowly dims. The air chills even more and the nights get longer, the sun weaker and more distant, drawing its warmth away. The cold air is a reminder to hunker down, to rest. Snow piles high on the sides of the streets, banks towering over dog walkers as they struggle in the ruts. Dawn dreads the long nights, the darkness that feels alive suddenly with malicious possibilities, the darkness outside her bedroom window like a physical presence. She can't tell if it's beckoning to her or mocking her. Maybe both. She feels strangely distant, like there's a layer of gauze between her and the world.

Being in the house these days feels like it did when she was young, and she worries that the two realities are becoming confused, entwined. The then and the now. The here and the gone. At certain times of day, it feels extremely likely that she will find Violet in bed in the back room, alive but dying. She will find herself flung back to a time when her world was insular, just her and her brother, with their parents orbiting in the distance.

As little kids, Dawn and Cody played with their toy cars and stuffed animals under the sheet-draped dining room table. The sheets were a soft barrier between them and everything else. It felt safe in there, and secret, and fun. Cody made a stuffed walrus eat a handful of Dawn's toy cars, and Dawn burst into tears. Violet tossed a slipper at the sheets and shouted, "Stop crying or I'll take down the fort!" Cody scuttled out from under the sheet, grabbed one of Violet's slippers, and brought it back into the fort, hiding it as revenge. Violet pretended to limp around looking for it and they stifled giggles, then shrieked when she threw open the sheet doorway.

They sat side by side on the couch, watching some cartoon on TV. Violet was sitting on the floor in between them, leaning back against the couch. Dawn and Cody both had long lengths of Violet's black hair in their hands, dividing their sections into three equal portions, then winding them together. Both children silently braided their mother's hair, small hands quick and confident, glancing down at their work, then up at the TV, like old women weaving or sewing or beading in front of their shows. The braids were lopsided and a bit messy, but Violet said they were great anyway, though she didn't keep them in for very long. Both children were nearly breathless from the sustained close contact with their mother, with her hair at least. "Thanks for the braids, kids," she said, before she got up and left them.

Once, Cody tried to teach Dawn how to kick a soccer ball. They were in the scraggly field at the back of the park down the street from their house. It was overcast and no one else was there. They practised for a long time and she gradually got better at connecting with the ball with the top of her foot, not her toes. Cody clapped her on the back and ran a lap, yelling with his arms in the air, "I'm the world's greatest coach!" It started to rain lightly.

Preteen Cody pushed a shopping cart down the pasta aisle and Dawn searched the shelves for the sauce their mother liked. They shopped together in quiet companionship. Both of them liked being at the grocery store. They enjoyed the order of the shelves and aisles, the colourful packaging of the food, the pleasing arrangement of the fruit in the produce section. Martin, who hated to shop, gave them cash and sent them in with a list, then sat in the car in the parking lot with a book.

As teenagers, they passed each other in the hallway at school between classes, and Cody, with a group of friends, ignored Dawn, who was walking alone. Dawn pretended not to notice him.

Now, Dawn is drifting. She's been here before, free-floating through her life with nothing touching her, no pain and no joy. But this time she can sense something else, something deeper beneath the surface struggling to make itself known.

Something she can't quite access, some knowledge she is being prevented from knowing. The fabric of time, of reality around her, is stretching and thinning.

As she's wondering when she will crack, what part of her will burst open—heart? head?—Crystal calls.

"Wanna come over?" she says, like it hasn't been weeks since they've spoken. Hasn't it? Dawn feels like she's been in her room, alone, forever.

"What?" Dawn says.

"Wanna come over? Cody and Tyler are coming. We're gonna watch the game, eat some snacks, have some beer. Come on over!"

Dawn feels a sharp disorientation. "Okay. Be there in a bit."

She stares at the wall, at a pattern forming on the white paint, but when she squints, it turns out to be nothing. A trick of the eye. She should change, put on some nicer clothes. She's been in sweats for a while now. Her clothes are heaped in the dresser, spilling over the edges so the drawers can no longer be closed. She pulls a garment from the tangle of fabrics and holds up a black sweater dress, slightly pilled. She rubs with her thumb at a small stain of something gross and white. It's better than sweats.

She pulls a parka over the dress and stuffs her feet into the hard winter boots that she hates, that always seem to jam her ankle. Wraps a scarf around her face. She checks the fridge for beer, but it's already been ransacked by Cody or Tyler. She shrugs and heads out. Crystal said they had beer anyway. The walk is short, but there is a nip in the wind that freezes Dawn's exposed cheeks and eyes. A car honks as it passes her, going too fast.

The Reed household is two blocks away, just around a few corners. It's located on a new street, right at the seam where the old neighbourhood ends and the new development began a few years ago. The street marks the boundary where old becomes new—the road torn up and extended to accommodate the new homes. The Reeds live in a two-storey model with an attached garage. It's made of monotonous pale brick and grey stone, and the garage, a utilitarian double, is the focal point at the front of the house. Dawn thinks it's unbelievably ugly.

As she approaches the front door, two small faces appear in the big window next to it. The little boys stare mutely at her from behind the glass, and then one waves a small hand. She waves back, then rings the doorbell.

Crystal opens the door almost instantly and pulls Dawn inside, smiling widely. "Dawn! So good to see you. Come in, sweetheart, come in." The boys have disappeared elsewhere into the house. Dawn hugs Crystal uncomfortably and takes off her shoes.

Boring but immaculate from the outside, the new home is a mess inside. Dawn takes it in quickly as Crystal hangs her coat in an overflowing front closet. The staircase leading to the second floor is littered with clothes and toys. The open-concept main floor is similarly strewn. Added to the chaos are books, piles of papers, stained photo albums, file folders in teetering stacks all over the carpet. Every surface is covered with something, including a mound of half-folded clean laundry on one corner of the dark wood dining-room table. Electrical chargers sprout from the furniture, and a piano by the window the boys peered out of has almost been completely consumed by junk. There are heaps of brand-new clothes with the hangers and tags still on. There are similar piles of new shoes and toys.

Hoarder, Dawn thinks, staring around.

Crystal smiles tightly. A deep sadness and an odd, hunted quality play across her face at once. "They're gifts," she says, not meeting Dawn's eye. "Gifts for people's kids and stuff. You know, birthdays, Christmas, whatever!"

She reaches out a hand and lays it on a pink satin dress on top of a nearby stack. Her fingers stroke the soft fabric gently, and Dawn feels like she's witnessing something intimate and private. It's clear the clothes and toys and books will never be gifted, at least not at the rate they've been collected.

"That's nice," Dawn says noncommittally. "Nice to be prepared." She really, deeply doesn't want to get into it with Crystal.

Crystal beams at her like that's all the validation she'll ever need in her lifetime, and Dawn feels a stab of guilt that she brushes aside.

"Well, we're all downstairs, Dawn! Come on, follow me." Crystal leads her through the kitchen—Dawn gets the impression of crusted dishes and food everywhere—and then down a flight of stairs.

The stairs open onto a semi-finished basement. The corner with the furnace is all damp-looking concrete and pipes, but the other side of the room opens onto a good-sized rec area, carpeted and with insulated walls and ceiling. In sharp contrast to the rest of the house, the basement rec area is neat and tidy, with no toys or clothing in sight.

Dawn can see the back of Tyler, Cody, and Jake's heads—they're sitting in a row on a big brown suede couch facing the hockey game on a massive flat-screen TV. There's a low coffee table and an armchair. Some kind of framed plaque on the wall as the only nod to decor. Crystal's sons are standing off to the side of the couch, holding hands, transfixed by the enormous TV.

"They're not really allowed down here," Crystal says to Dawn over her shoulder. "It's really Daddy's space, you know?" Dawn flinches inwardly noting that Crystal is the type to refer to Jake as *Daddy* even when she's not addressing their kids.

Something objectionable happens in the game and all three men groan and shout in unison, a commercial for "Men Watching Sports." The boys reach out and clutch their mother's legs.

Jake notices them and cries, "Dawn!" throwing his arms in the air like they're old friends. "Grab a beer, grab a seat!"

Dawn takes a beer from the cooler beside the couch and plops into the armchair. She avoids making eye contact with Cody.

"How goes it, Dawn?" Tyler asks without taking his eyes off the screen.

"It goes fine," she says, cracking open her beer.

She finally looks over at her brother. He meets her eye and smiles. Dawn tries to remember the last time she saw him. She doesn't think he's been home for weeks, but she can't trust her memory lately. She's sure it's been a long time since she left him at the mall food court.

"How's it going, Dawn?" Cody asks easily, nudging Tyler to grab him another beer.

Tyler looks ... amused. The same look he wore after Cody hit him at the booze can—like it doesn't matter what's happening right now, because he knows what's going to happen. He's leaning back against the couch, body relaxed, looking from person to person, a lazy smile on his face. Dawn gets the distinct impression that he considers himself apart, separate from them, better in some way. There's a dangerous, ultimately reckless, feeling to him. As she watches Tyler, just for a second, his image flutters, like a bad signal. Dawn glances over at the game, men zipping around the ice in HD, every line crisp and sharp. Her stomach clenches.

"It's going good," she says evenly.

"Cool," he says. There's a quick, mean set to Cody's mouth, there for an instant and then gone, as he looks toward the action on the screen.

Jake's booming voice cuts above the volume of the television before she can think of a reply to keep the conversation going.

"Dawn, dear Dawn," Jake says, smiling lazily at her through hooded eyes. "Who's your team? Who're you cheering for?"

It's only late afternoon, but Jake is clearly drunk, betrayed by the thick slur he's fighting to keep out of his speech. There's a stiffness to Cody as he sits next to Jake, a tension that permeates his whole body.

"Neither," she says. "Both their jerseys are ugly."

Jake laughs far too loudly. When his laughter dies down the basement is quiet but for a blaring car commercial, and Dawn feels the pulse of a headache beginning in the base of her skull.

"Should I go get some snacks together?" Crystal interjects.

"I'll help you," Dawn says and springs from the chair, not wanting to be left alone with the men.

Dawn and Crystal herd the boys up the stairs. Dawn hangs back by the kitchen table and adopts more of a supervisory role in preparing the snacks. The two boys rush the fridge, throwing it open and pointing out what they want to eat in high-pitched voices, tugging at their mom's leggings. Crystal grabs various tubs and packages and piles them on a section of counter that she's cleared by moving everything on it to the floor. As Crystal puts crackers and baby carrots and cheese on a large plastic tray, Dawn notices the tight hunch of her shoulders. Crystal brings the tray over to the kitchen table, and then grabs a bottle of vodka out of the cupboard.

"Let's have some Caesars!" she declares. "I'm sick of beer."

She roots through the fridge for the Clamato juice, and Dawn hands each boy a piece of cheese from the platter. They eat the cheese and say nothing, looking at each other instead of at her.

Weird kids, she thinks, as Crystal returns to the table with two tumblers. The thought of the vodka creates an oily feeling in Dawn's stomach. She watches Crystal make the drinks and searches her profile for the little girl she grew up with. In adulthood, Crystal's face has hardened, its angles sharpened. When Crystal tucks her hair behind her ear, Dawn can see the line of her spray tan—an unnatural tawny brown that turns suddenly to pale white.

Crystal hands Dawn a Caesar, and they clink glasses. The drink is spicy and strong. The pounding in Dawn's head is growing by the minute. Crystal seems fragile, needy, in her messy kitchen, making a plate of snacks for her husband downstairs, and Dawn realizes this might be her last chance to get someone to tell her what's going on, her last chance to know.

"Hey, Crystal. Can I ask you something?"

"Sure, Dawn. What's up?"

Crystal adds another pour of vodka to her drink, giving a Dawn a conspiratorial wink. The sun is starting to set outside the kitchen windows, the violet gloaming of dusk bringing a tightness to Dawn's chest.

"What's happening, Crystal? What are Cody and Tyler up to?"

Crystal's face tightens like a snare. Dawn locks her gaze onto Crystal's, searching the blue eyes that are wheeling through emotions, flashing with panic, anger, calculation. After a few seconds they come to rest: blank and unreadable. Her face slackens.

"What do you mean, Dawn?"

Crystal's voice is devoid of emotion, of inflection. She's looking through Dawn now. Dawn blanches and takes a step back from the table, noticing how closely they've been huddled together. Crystal's sons are standing a few feet away, watching them talk, their arms wrapped around each other.

"I ..." Dawn glances at the kids, then leans forward again, closing the gap she'd put between them, and whispers quickly, "You can tell me, Crystal. Maybe I can help. Help you? Tell me what's going on. Are you okay?"

Dawn can sense a river in Crystal, waiting to be undammed. There's a part of Crystal that very desperately wants to tell. But Crystal fights that part into submission. She says in a clear, concerned tone, "Nothing's going on, Dawn. Are you okay, honey?"

Dawn takes a step back again, then nods, picks up her drink, and takes a long sip to cover her silence.

Crystal watches her for a moment, then smiles. "Okay, then." She already has the platter of snacks hoisted on one hip, her drink in the other hand, and is heading toward the basement stairs.

Heat rises in Dawn's body, a mixture of fear and that other, snakelike thing—shame. The mere insinuation that there might be something wrong with her is enough for the shame to rise. The deep, unshakable shame that has repeatedly sunk her shoulders low since childhood the way it permanently sunk Violet's, and Cody's, though he jacked his back up with anger. She aches with it, its roots shooting all the way through her, a knot tangled within her very being.

That knot tightened after Cody was sent to prison. It was the real reason she didn't visit her brother for seven years. Not fear, not anger. Shame. The face-burning, shrinking shame that Cody had become all the worst things their neighbours had whispered about him when he was a teenager. She didn't spend those long years he was in prison wondering how her brother could have done it. She spent those years refusing to think about it and wondering how her brother could have done that to her.

She worried that every time someone looked at her, they now saw her brother instead, worried that she'd become inextricably linked with what Cody did.

She often thinks about that last minute, before the irreversible was done. That last minute before their lives changed, shattered, and reformed into twisted patterns. At the centre of her own crooked pattern, she's still standing in that back lane.

It's a long time to be out in the cold.

Her headache has consumed the entirety of her skull now, a persistent throbbing pain that emanates from everywhere at once. She grips the table, pressing the edge painfully into her palms, before grabbing her drink and following Crystal and the boys downstairs.

The men are gathered around the low coffee table in front of the huge TV, a white-haired announcer bleating over a purple tie covered in green avocados on the screen in front of them. The garish man is leering over them, angling down to watch what they're doing. He shouts angrily about a second-period play and slams down a hammy fist. The men at the table don't look up. They're absorbed in a scattering of papers, heads bent low to examine them. Jake reaches out and underlines something on a page with his finger, jabs at it. Cody and Tyler glance at each other and nod solemnly, like soldiers receiving orders from their superior officer. But there's a shadow of a smile on Tyler's lips, like he's enjoying himself, possibly at Jake's expense.

"Snacks!" Crystal sing-songs in a voice so clear and sharp it could cut glass.

The men whirl to face them like off-tempo dancers. Jake gathers the papers into a pile and slides them under the couch in a way that does not imply urgency.

Crystal deposits the platter of snacks on the cleared table and heaps chips and veggie sticks onto two paper plates for the boys. The precarious arrangement of carrots and cucumbers on one plate tumbles onto the table and carpet. A rigidity comes over Jake's face as he stares at his wife, plain contempt in his cold eyes. The transformation is instant and complete. The hardness is not a shell or a shield but a parting that reveals the foundation underneath. Something in him surges forth and is laid bare on his face as he looks at Crystal and the fallen vegetables. His upper lip curls and his eyes say *useless*, say *hate*, but his mouth says nothing. Crystal rushes to put the veggies back on the plate and casts a quick, surreptitious glance at her husband.

Dawn's drink tastes suddenly bitter in her mouth. She takes one more sip and puts it down. Crystal sits cross-legged on the floor with her sons, eating a carrot stick.

Dawn stands stiffly, pretending to watch the game. Two men on the screen throw their gloves and helmets to the ice and swing clumsily at each other, spinning in circles on their skates. There's a stillness in the basement, a stillness over all of them, like a tomb. They watch the rest of the game in silence.

When it's over, Jake looks around at everyone for the first time in half an hour, claps his big hands together once, firmly, and says in a tone of forced joviality, "Well, what a game, eh?"

The spell breaks.

The boys hang off Tyler's knees, asking him questions, and Crystal, Jake, and Cody sit on the couch, talking animatedly now. Jake's hand is on Crystal's thigh, his thumb restlessly rubbing the black cotton of her leggings.

Dawn clears her throat, but no one looks up. She feels distinctly ... unwanted. Which is strange because Crystal invited her over. But it feels like she's intruding on a club with an exclusive membership.

Finally, she says, "Guess I'll get going now," too loud, a weird, tight smile on her face. For some reason, she nods her head in affirmation of her own words.

Everyone is looking at her. Crystal stands up and extends her arms, palms upward. She smiles. "Thanks for coming, Dawn."

Dawn nods again. "You're staying?" she asks Cody, and he raises a hand to say goodbye. He barely looks at her and doesn't stop talking to Tyler in a quick whisper. Tyler also lifts an indifferent hand.

Jake, though, stands up and walks over to her. She's afraid he's going to hug her, pull her against his large, somewhat doughy frame, and she'll be forced to inhale the stale sweat smell of his T-shirt, the tang of his skin, the musk from his underarms. He grabs her lightly by her upper arms and looks directly into her eyes.

"Take care now, Dawn." His voice is pitched low, authoritative. He's commanding her to take care.

She stares into his eyes. If they are windows, she doesn't know what they look upon. There's a cipher in his gaze she can't interpret, but it stirs an unpleasant buzzing, low inside her, a whirring and clicking.

She steps back. "Thanks, Jake. Uh, thanks for having me over. See ya, I guess." She keeps backing up as she speaks, and she flashes back to the barbecue in Mrs. Cleary's backyard. A mirror image of her backing away, retreating. But if she keeps backing up, she knows she'll only circle back around.

The desire to be gone, to be anywhere else, comes on so strongly that Dawn feels faint, like some part of her has already broken loose and left. She wants to leave. Not just the Reeds' house but South Saint Jude, the city. She should never have come back here.

What would her life be like if she hadn't ever left? Maybe she and Crystal would take their kids to the same park, with a new plastic play structure, they'd played at as kids, shop at the newly renovated Safeway down the street. This vision can't really take hold, though, because Dawn knows with certainty that it never could have been. Since she was a teenager, she'd known that settling down and staying here was not something she wanted. The thought of this, in fact, filled her with a fluttery panic. Her body responded by saying, urgently, *Don't get trapped, get out*, and she never stopped to ask, *Trapped by what?*

So, she left. She'd moved to the grey steel-and-glass heights of Toronto, a city that sprawled upwards rather than out. Out like the long, low prairies, like loneliness lapping at the edges, like empty fields of wheat. She'd hoped that a different place would make her different, that she could remake herself into someone new, half-believing in that old promise that in a big city you can be anyone you want to be.

But she didn't become someone new; she didn't become anybody she wanted to be. She remained herself, still carrying around the same aching heart.

CHAPTER FIFTEEN

The days are all washed out with pale light, slow and strange.

Everything's wrong, but Dawn can't leave. Despite what Cody said at the mall. Despite her fear, despite the burning need in her to run. She should be here—she can feel that in her quivering bones now. She's brought this on, whatever it turns out to be. It sought her out because it knew who she really was inside. She deserves this. She doesn't deserve to escape. A heavy listlessness settles in her, making her limbs, her body, harder to move freely and making her mind accept the heaviness. Vague thoughts of leaving, of finding help, somewhere, somehow, slide off the surface of her mind, refusing to take hold anymore.

She should accept this, whatever it is.

Cody and Tyler skulk around in grim moods and spend an increasing amount of time in the garage. She doesn't join them anymore. Martin and Tyler and Cody orbit around her, and she is sometimes aware of them and sometimes not.

Out of nowhere, her dad begins to plan what he's calling a "Bucket List Road Trip" through California. Cody and Tyler encourage him, sitting with Martin at the kitchen table evening after evening, scrolling through camping gear on his old iPad.

Camping? Dawn wonders whether she or her father is living in the wrong reality.

Tyler zooms in on a one-man tent, a technical-looking nylon sheath that Dawn's pretty sure is meant for hardcore hikers, highlighting a feature for Martin, who nods along, eyes only half focused. Cody's staring at the door, but really at nothing, and his breathing is shallow, like he can't completely draw a full breath.

Dawn sits numbly at the kitchen table as Martin shows her brochure after glossy brochure for various landmarks and major attractions along his route. She has no idea where he's gotten them from, but there are several scattered around now. She stares at the pictures of aspirational vineyards and awe-inspiring mountain vistas and kitschy American roadside attractions and tries to imagine these are real places, where real people go. She nods at what her father tells her. Her head feels like it weighs thirty pounds. Each nod takes a concentrated effort.

"Since when have you wanted to go on a road trip to California?" she asks, her voice worryingly quiet and scratchy, like she hasn't used it for a while. Her voice sounds like Violet's.

She can tell as soon as she's spoken that she's interrupted him, but this question feels important.

"Since always," Martin says, looking at her askance. "Since always, honey."

"In the middle of winter?"

"It's an adventure." He smiles at her reassuringly.

Dawn shuts her eyes, wonders if she's still in bed, dreaming. She wishes she could shed her skin, slip away from herself.

Dawn opens her eyes and she's alone at the kitchen table, the room silent but for the erratic hum of the refrigerator and her breathing, hitching audibly in her throat. She seems to be spending a lot of time sitting alone in the kitchen on their hard-backed wooden chairs. She stares at her hands clasped before her, or at the wall, and sometimes she swears there's someone in her peripheral vision in the chair beside her, a flicker of jeans. She wants to reach out her hand, but when she moves the flicker is always gone. She's never able to take his hand.

MARTIN LEAVES ON a sleet-grey morning. He packs his truck as Dawn stands on the front lawn in an open parka, her arms crossed obstinately over her chest. She does not help him load his suitcase or road snacks. Her head is throbbing, this constant accompaniment of pain she's had for...she doesn't know how long now. The fog around her is getting thicker, slowing her more, and everyone else is still moving at normal speed.

Martin wraps his arms around her, briefly and awkwardly. It is the first time they've hugged in years and Dawn's body rejects the experience, remaining stiff and disbelieving. He lets go and takes a step back.

"Bye, kiddo. See you in a few weeks."

"Are you going to say bye to Cody?"

"I already did this morning. He had to run out for something."

A frown tugs at the corners of Dawn's mouth. Martin looks away and shrugs in response to some unasked question. He smiles at her, and then gets in his truck.

"Are you sure it's fine to go in winter?" she calls out, a sudden burst of anxiety blooming in her chest. There's something else she should have said, like having somebody's name on the tip of your tongue, but she feels it fall further away, out of her grasp, and she blinks and she's freezing cold, the wind whipping through her open jacket, and Martin's truck is gone from the curb.

The house is full of the kind of silence before something happens.

The air is dry and there's a faint, strange crackle to it, like electricity. Dawn looks around the kitchen and notes—with faint pleasure quickly swallowed by the fog—that it's clean and still fairly organized. The windows in the living room have been washed, and the cold winter light that comes in seems unreal, beamed from another plane.

She puts coffee on and sits at the kitchen table waiting for it to finish, flipping over a newspaper so she won't see the headlines. She puts her face in her hands, feels the greasiness of her palms against the skin of her cheeks and makes herself endure it. She digs her fingernails into her forehead.

The coffee machine beeps.

She drinks two cups and can't remember doing it.

The air crackles around her.

She realizes her cup has been empty for a while. She stands up and feels a resolution forming—seizing on an internal spark of motion, she forces herself to grab her car keys and move to the door. She shouldn't just be sitting here waiting, should she? She doesn't know what she's waiting for.

Dawn drives north into the city, taking the highway that carries her past the familiar low-slung buildings on the left, the partially frozen river to the right. The fog seems to thin by degrees the farther she travels from the house, though never releases her entirely. She doesn't know where she's heading until she sees her old red-brick high school up ahead.

She parks in the staff parking lot behind the building, sits in her car, and stares at the rows of blank windows.

Is it closed for the holidays? Is it a weekend?

She is removed from space and time.

The high school has a bright new digital sign, currently

flashing a pixelated image of the school's mascot, Bennie the Bulldog, and it's been painted recently, its turquoise trim spruced up. She can remember so vividly what it was like to walk down the school's halls from class to class, to pass the days inside crowded classrooms, to talk to almost no one. Strange that such a blur of an experience can remain so clear in her mind. That lonely, desolate stretch of time. The sensation of being unseen, unknown. A ghost, like her mother.

One spring day, Dawn walked to the nearby bagel place and got a sandwich for lunch. Even though there was still a bite to the air, the sun was out and getting stronger, so she was planning to eat it at one of the faded green picnic benches that dotted the school's back field. A group of students was standing in the field in a rough circle.

Dawn wove around a few people until she could see the centre of the circle, where two people were grappling on the ground. She froze mid-bite of her bagel when she realized that one of the two people, the one on top who was hammering his fist into the other one's face, was Cody. His fist flew back and connected, flew back and connected. Dawn was terrified her brother would kill the other kid. But then he heaved himself off and walked away, the crowd quickly parting for him as he moved through, his hands on the back of his head, breathing hard.

She learned through the school grapevine that the other kid had come up to Cody, apparently on a dare, and asked him if he drank Listerine like "all the other dirty savages." And so that was that. He'd ended up with a broken nose, a fractured cheekbone, and two extremely painful-looking black eyes. He told his parents it had been much more of an even battle than it had been, and they didn't press charges. She knew the kid deserved to get hit for what he'd said; that wasn't what scared her. It was the look she'd seen on her brother's face, the intense frenzy of his punches, like he wasn't going to quit until the person under him was dead. In that moment, she'd seen the stopper on his rage come off, or thought she had, and she worried about what would happen when he wasn't able to put it back on again.

But she didn't allow herself to go there, not then. It was too horrible to even think about.

Dawn looks outside and it's nighttime.

The day has dissolved around her. The inside of the car is freezing cold. The engine is off and apparently has been for some time. Her breath clouds the air. She's in the driver's seat, still strapped in, her hands like claws around the wheel. She painfully unclamps them and starts the car, shivering. She presses her forehead against the cool leather of the steering wheel.

Now, when she looks at her brother, she sees another trembling image superimposed over him. She doesn't think she'll ever be able to look at him again and see only him. Only the boy she's known her entire life, the boy who brought her sandwiches as their mom died, the boy who would read beside her on weekend afternoons, both of them on the floor in a patch of sunlight. The boy who grew into an angry teen, and then an angry man. Whose sorrow metastasized into rage and consumed him. That angry man is all she'll ever really see now, even if he's laughing with his mouth wide and head thrown back. She cannot visit that boy anymore. Even in her dreams, she returns only to that night, to that back lane. Every memory washed with red.

She raises her head from the wheel. She turns the heat as high as it will go and wraps her arms around herself, jiggling her legs furiously up and down, until she's finally warm enough to drive. She puts the car in reverse, and as she swings it around, her headlights pass over the fence, low wooden posts with a thick chain strung between them.

She thinks she sees a figure crouching there on the chain. Not a human figure but one with thick, short fur. A glimpse of huge paws.

She drives out of the lot and doesn't look in the rear-view mirror.

The sign flashes and the affable face of Bennie the Bulldog transforms; the dog is frothing at the mouth, snarling, its lips curled back—it flashes back to normal.

She drives the highway north.

She passes an apartment building where a cluster of people are outside on the sidewalk, staring up at the roof. An old woman is hugging a little girl close to her, others huddle around them, and one woman is pointing up. Dawn swerves into the next lane as she tries to catch sight of what they're looking at, but she can't see anything. She concentrates on the road again.

She passes a tattoo parlour with a huge well-lit front window and a black faux-Gothic sign that says *Meditate &*

Mayhem. As she cruises by, she's certain she sees Crystal in the window, her blond hair in disarray and eyes roving. Her hands are raised in front of her and moving in strange, slow motions, like she's casting a spell. Her fingernails tap against the glass. Dawn looks back at the road, then quickly back at the shop as it passes out of sight. The front window is empty.

Ten minutes later, she turns off into a section of residential roads. The moon hangs low in the sky, its bright white belly distended. Moonlight creeps between the houses, silvery and pale. She comes quietly to a stop in front of the two-storey clapboard house with a small front porch crowded with the type of debris that accumulates over a lifetime: a sunken couch piled high with winter coats, three bicycles in various states of decomposition, a rusted metal ladder, and stacks of magazines bound together with twine.

She's back at the booze can.

She thinks of all the people who pass through this house, looking for an illicit party, for company. For something darker. Flash of a face from a billboard, flash of a girl leaving a party alone. That Venn diagram so many navigate—pleasure and danger, the two circles overlapping at the centre for some.

Is there an answer to be found here?

She feels herself moving through space thick as honey, dragging her limbs, forging onward. Her head hurts like a thousand feet are trampling through it. It can take a lifetime to piece things together. Whatever her brother's put in motion, whatever he and Tyler are plotting—she can still try. Maybe it can be stopped, despite this feeling dragging her down.

Her limbs move through the fog. She gets out of the car and heads around the house to the back door.

CHAPTER SIXTEEN

As Dawn walks along the side of the house, the heavy moon hides behind a dark streak of cloud. It's bitterly cold. The air bites at her lungs. The snowy ground before her swells and dips. In the darkness, it shimmers, changes into the snow from years ago. There are patches of red on the ground, whorls of footprints. She stops walking. She won't follow those footprints.

It's only a short stretch to the back of the house, but she cannot see the end of this dark tunnel she's in. The moonlight returns, a soft pool of light over by the fence.

It illuminates the coarse fur of a massive hare, a jack-rabbit, bigger than any Dawn has seen before. Even as the rabbit sits still in the moonlight, something ripples below its fur, beneath its surface. Its feet are huge, and its ears, long and velveteen, lie down along its broad back. Facing Dawn, its eyes are pure blackness, two absences of light. As she watches, her back pressed to the side of the house, it tilts its head, like its listening to something.

A charge in the air prickles and snaps, crackles out a message Dawn can't decipher. Bathed in light, the rabbit rises to stand on two legs. It's nearly as tall as a person. The front legs and paws dangle in front of its chest, like its limp body is being held up on strings. Pulled up. And then it starts to move toward her. It moves in lurching steps, each hind limb yanked forward in turn. The light travels with it across the snow, toward her. A grinding, hissing noise fills the dark, a buzz, and the great hare advances jerkily, and the stars have been put out, *Oh, it's coming—*

A bright beam of light compels Dawn to open her tightly shut eyes. Mickey stands at the corner of the house, shining a flashlight on the spot where the rabbit had just been. The space is empty. Dawn's breathing is heavy and ragged.

"For some reason, this works," Mickey says, holding up the big yellow flashlight. Then she says, "Come inside," and pushes Dawn ahead of her through the open back door.

In the kitchen an elderly woman with a very white powdered face and bright lipstick, her blue-tinted hair in a beehive, is pouring herself a mug of whisky. She glances up guiltily as Dawn and Mickey enter.

"'Fuck outta here, Doris!" Mickey hollers, and the woman giggles gleefully and flees down the basement stairs. Mickey stomps over and slams the door shut. The muffled sounds of music and people can still be heard through the kitchen floor and cigarette smoke laces the air. Dawn fights to slow her breathing.

Mickey grabs the whisky and two mugs and turns to Dawn. "I remember you. Let's go to my room."

Dawn follows mutely, like a child being told what to do. Mickey's room is through a formal dining room, with a stately wood table stationed in the middle and surrounded by eight chairs stifled by thick yellowing dustcovers, and up a flight of stairs. It's spacious and full of an odd assortment of vintage furniture: a pink-and-gold printed screen draped with silk scarves and clothes, a four-poster dark wood bed-frame, a velvet armchair with books on its seat. Knick-knacks and porcelain dolls cover the wood end tables and the dresser that hulks in the corner. There's an all-purple ensuite bathroom with no apparent door and heavy dark-blue velvet curtains blocking out the window.

Mickey motions for Dawn to sit on the bed—a big, slightly musty king bed with layers of duvets, afghans, and sheets in a tangled but inviting nest. Dawn smooths down some of the blankets and perches on the edge.

Mickey pours whisky into the mugs and hands one to Dawn, who doesn't want it but takes a gulp anyway.

"Cody's sister, yeah? You guys came here a while back and had to go for fighting?"

"Uh, yeah." Dawn is suddenly nervous. She kicks herself for only feeling that way now.

"It's okay," Mickey adds quickly. "Just making sure." She

laughs, a gravelly baritone. "I was pretty fucked up that night. Sometimes I like to party, I like to partake. You can't run a place like this and not get down and dirty once in a while." She laughs again and takes a huge slug of whisky.

Then she asks, "What did you see out there, Dawn?"

Dawn doesn't look at her, scans the bric-a-brac of the room instead. Dawn is not in the habit of trusting people she doesn't know. Still, Mickey saved her—saved her from what, Dawn can't say.

"I saw…a rabbit. Like, a huge fucking jackrabbit. By the fence. It was just sitting there looking at me, and then it stood up. And it was walking toward me, but it didn't look like it was walking on its own, and I know this sounds dumb, but just the way it moved was so…so…awful." She glances over at Mickey.

Mickey meets her eyes and nods. "I saw you through the side window. I don't know what it is," she says, "but it comes around sometimes. Different people can see it. It looks like different things, too. There's a weird energy around it, right? A weird vibe. I don't like to mess too deeply with that kind of stuff. Anyway, I figured out one night by accident that shining a flashlight on it makes it disappear."

"What happens if it doesn't disappear? If it…catches someone?"

"Oh, sweetie, don't think about that. Maybe it's not trying to catch anyone. Not that I'm gonna find out."

Dawn finishes her drink. "I came here for a reason," she says, and Mickey claps her hands delightedly. "A mission!"

she crows. "All deals done on the low, honey. Use the back room. Ask for Dean."

Dawn half-smiles. "No. Thanks, though. My brother, last time we were here—he said he was grabbing something off someone, and it was this piece of paper with, like, instructions written on it. I need to find out what it is, what it means."

"Instructions?" Mickey wrinkles her nose. "Instructions for what?"

"That's what I want to find out. It said something like: *nighttime, full moon, winter*. Any idea what that could mean?"

Mickey smirks. "Sounds like a poem. I don't know what that means, love, terribly sorry. I should get back to my patrons. Just wanted to make sure you were all right." She places a hand, her wrist covered in brass bangles, on Dawn's.

"Do you mind if I ask around a bit downstairs?" Dawn says.

Mickey's eyes flicker ever so quickly, but she smiles and says, "Of course not, dear."

As they leave the room, Dawn turns to Mickey. "What did you see? Out there?"

Mickey pulls her bedroom door shut with a neat click. "Nothing, hon. I never see anything."

IT'S NOT NEARLY as busy as last time Dawn was here. She decides that blending in—"partaking," in Mickey's words—will get her further than if she's stone cold sober.

She leans casually on the bar and orders a shot and a beer. *Fuck it.* The shot goes down better than the whisky in Mickey's bedroom. She tips the bartender, who's blasting the Germs through a shitty speaker system.

A woman with a tangle of chocolate-brown curls and smudged eyeliner is sitting in the corner with a child, around ten years old, and a white husky on a chain. Small and grave, the child watches Dawn, unblinking. The husky is sleeping, unperturbed, its paws twitching. The woman nods sagely as the child leans over and whispers in her ear.

Dawn makes her way to the back room of low-slung furniture. The walls, she notices this time, are covered in red striped wallpaper and hung with psychedelic paintings in swirling neon colours that hurt to look at too long. In the same brown chair as before sits the man Tyler was talking to that night. Dawn plunks down on the couch next to him, trying to seem casual.

"Hey, Paul, right? I think I remember you from the other night. My name's Dawn. You might know my friend Tyler?"

The man is made of right angles: his copper-brown skin, sallow now in the winter, pulled over sharpness and points. He looks like a man who doesn't cuddle, never allows himself to soften. He's of average build but has huge hands, callused, and Dawn wonders what he chooses to use them for.

His eyes slide over to Dawn's, and he nods once. "I know him. Remember you."

Dawn sips her beer and wonders what to ask, but Paul speaks again before she can figure it out.

Looking off across the room, rather than at her, like he really doesn't want to be having this conversation, he says, "Don't play with things you don't understand. That's a good lesson to learn."

"Me? What am I playing with?" she asks.

Paul stares at her head-on. He's not appraising her; he looks like he already knows her, like he understands something essential about her, something she doesn't.

"I can't help you," he says firmly, and Dawn feels desperation rise.

"Can't or won't?" she asks and sits staring at him for long seconds, but he doesn't answer her. The air is so thick with smoke that Dawn struggles to pull in a full breath. Underneath the smoke is a sharp, crisp smell like sea salt. She can taste it on her tongue. Dawn downs the rest of her beer in two gulps and sets it on the side table.

"You should go now," he says, more like he's resigned than angry, and Dawn feels a draining away inside of her. She suddenly becomes aware of the other people in the room, who have stopped talking and are now watching them.

She gets up to leave, and as she's walking away, he says to her back, "You won't stop it. It started a long time ago."

His words follow her out of the room.

Chunks of time slide away from her like ice shearing off a glacier.

She's suddenly outside in the bitter wind, jacket and

shoes undone, unlocking her car door. She slides into the car and starts the engine, hugging herself to warm up. The house looks dormant from the front, unremarkable, yet it seems to emit a call into the night. There's no way to know who will hear it.

She turns on the radio. There are almost no other cars on the road and no one out on the sidewalks. A cold, charged stillness all around.

Her mind won't stop returning to the rabbit in the moonlight, the bloody prints in that old snow.

The fog begins to constrict around her. Chaos, obliteration, lick at her edges.

She drives home like she's being fast-forwarded through time, dragged forward.

She's in her driveway and the radio is playing.

A song ends, and in the moment of static silence before another plays, a voice speaks into the dark of the car.

"Don't leave," Violet says.

CHAPTER SEVENTEEN

The morning is cold and Dawn only half-wakes to it, chilly under the covers. Her room wavers in the winter light. She's reluctant to get up. It doesn't seem like much good can come from getting up. The fear in Dawn's chest expands to the rest of her body like a virus. Eating away at her edges, fraying her nerves, confusing her. She sees that cursed rabbit in her dreams and wakes up soaking in so much sweat that she starts to worry she's terminally ill. She throws off the cold, wet sheets and shimmies over on the bed until she's pressed up against the wall, smooths the sheet out around the crumpled, damp area where her dreaming body lay. *Absurd to be afraid of a rabbit*, she tries to tell herself. But deep down, in the place where her dreams come from, she knows it's not really a rabbit.

Something's building—something's coming. The nauseating cold knowing envelops her. It's coming and it's going to get her.

The remnants of last night's fragmented nightmare fall away as she fully opens her eyes and accepts that she's awake. Each night bleeds into the next morning, and afternoon, and evening. The boundary between night and day, waking and sleeping, is wearing thinner and thinner. Sometimes she swears she gets up, but the next thing she knows she's back in the bed. What will it mean when the boundaries blur completely and erase? Is it a dream world she'll inhabit or someplace else? When she closes her eyes, there's a pattern on the back of her eyelids, an intricately laced web; it spreads out, fungal, on the blank walls, too, when she stares at them, and all along the ceiling. It's been there for a while now.

She's not sure what day of the week it is, or how long Martin's been gone, though she vaguely remembers watching him pull away. There's a milky quality to the light lately that she doesn't like. It repulses her. She mostly stays in bed, huddled against the light under her covers, the small of her back aching, crying out in protest of her inertia. She's sure her brain is withering inside her skull, and this is what causes the terrible pains in her head. Her stomach churns, and she decides she should get some toast to settle it. She can move for that. It's a simple task. *And when did I last eat?* she wonders groggily.

She hauls herself out of bed and sits on the edge, half-dazed with the effort. She's not sure how long she's gone for, but she comes to swaying in place, still sitting on the edge of the bed, and her hands are clenching the bedsheets, and they feel sore from the effort.

She needs toast, she needs to eat.

She makes it to the kitchen by keeping her focus on toast, and is unnerved by the silence of the house, an expectant silence. She devours two pieces of buttered toast, hovering over the toaster until they pop, anxiety mounting the whole time. It feels safer to be in bed. As she's returning to her room, she sees Cody.

He's sitting in the living room, smack in the centre of the couch, staring at the dark screen of the television. There's a drunken slackness to his face, but his eyes are laser focused.

She walks toward him. "Cody?"

He doesn't respond.

"Cody?" she tries again louder.

No reaction.

"Cody!" She shouts it this time.

Her brother's limp posture and sharp gaze don't change.

She uses all her effort to raise a heavy arm and slap him, hard. The impact makes a clear sound in the quiet room.

Cody blinks and his eyes change instantly. He looks at her and she immediately goes still, like prey being sighted. The rage in his eyes would obliterate her.

Then, it's gone. And he looks nothing but drunk.

He stares blearily up at her. "Dawn? What's up?"

He licks his lips slowly and looks around the room like he's just realized where he is. "Fucked it up," he mutters and takes his head in his hands.

"What, Cody? What did you fuck up?"

She yells at her sluggish, muted self to pay attention through the fog, that this is important.

A sudden movement in the front yard pulls her eye toward the window, and she spins to face it, heart hammering. She scans the yard, but there's nothing there. Only branches swaying in the wind.

She turns back toward the couch and—

It's empty.

Must have gone out, she thinks, but wasn't he going to tell her something? She can't remember. She can't remember what she's doing up; she looks out the front window and the last of the setting sun is fading into night.

She goes to the kitchen and leans over the sink, drinks water straight from the tap. She should really get back to bed.

She straightens up and the sun streaming through the kitchen window makes her squint. It looks like a crisp, bright day. She shuffles back toward her bedroom. Back to sleep.

WHEN IT'S EXTREMELY cold out the thin layer of ice atop the snow glimmers and glints where the light catches it. It throws back blinding sunshine during the day. At night, it sparks and winks where the moonlight touches its peaks, sparkles in smooth blankets where the light falls in silver pools. It's enchanting, this lunar landscape of snow. Its beauty a muffler on the earth. It asks for stillness, demands it if it isn't given willingly.

Dawn is still.

Like snow has settled inside her, too, muting her thoughts. Something is calling to her from underneath the muffling within her, but she doesn't know what it's saying.

Time collapses. It's daylight and she shuts her eyes for a moment and when she opens them again a winter sunset replaces the night: fingers of dark violet clouds reach across the sky, a fading pale blue, their edges kissed with neon pinks and oranges.

Everywhere is dry and cold, and spring is so distant as to not exist.

Dawn starts to sleepwalk.

She rises and walks. Sometimes she thinks she's walking through winding underground corridors, pacing an entombed labyrinth. Rises and walks, and then wakes, confused, not underground but still buried.

She sleepwalked for a while shortly after Violet died. She always ends up in the same place now. She wakes, night after night, standing in the living room, in front of the window, facing the dark, empty street.

Then, one night, the street is not empty.

Dawn wakes with a full bladder. It presses painfully and urgently. She looks out the window. Standing very still in the centre of the street, a figure is facing her. Looking back at her.

Her bladder releases.

As the hot urine spills down her leg, she registers that the figure in the street is Crystal.

Crystal walks forward, with an odd, stiff gait, across the front lawn, coming closer to the house, to the window.

And as she approaches, Dawn sees that Crystal's face looks like it's been put together wrong.

The skin is stretched over bones that are misshapen and oddly sized, cheekbones huge and jutting, jaw grotesquely elongated. The eyes are sightless pools, receding into sockets that bulge outward.

The jaw begins to fall off, to drop toward the ground, and Dawn shouts and closes her eyes instinctively, afraid to see the tongue lolling in the ruined maw. She squeezes her eyes shut, but panic quickly forces her to open them again.

And Crystal is fine.

She immediately begins to back up, looking alarmed at finding herself where she is, shaking her head. Then she turns and runs off down the quiet street. Dawn's urine-soaked pants are freezing to her legs. She is shaking, too, with cold and with fear.

As Crystal runs away, Dawn sees that she isn't wearing any shoes, her bare feet slapping against the icy, hard ground.

TIME FLOWS AND pours over itself like mercury.

Dawn sleeps and wakes.

More people come to stand outside the house at night.

The short man from the living room that dizzying,

altering night—he comes. He stands behind the light of the street lamp, his face partly in shadow; still, she can see that it flickers, rearranges. Jake Reed appears one night, wearing a fixed smile like a rictus. He stands in the light and the loathsome smile never leaves his face.

Dawn wakes from her restless dreams and matches their gazes. She watches them as they watch her, and minutes slip by, or hours, or days, and it seems that something is closing in on her.

She wakes up swaying in the living room, in the spot where the black hole was opened.

Then Dawn hears something in the middle of the night and wakes in her bed, the sound lost immediately after she's heard it. A bone-deep, irresistible pull near her navel tells her she must get up and follow the already-forgotten sound.

She swings her legs out of bed and the air that greets her shins is frigid. There is a shimmer to the air, like an oil slick. Her toes are so cold they're already going numb. Shivering, she turns to search for her slippers and pulls up short. Her boots, thick wool socks hanging out of them, are lined up next to the bed. Her slippers are nowhere in sight.

She opens her door but doesn't move.

She doesn't want to walk down the hall.

The oil-slick air shakes and shimmers like a curtain, a veil of fine, fine crystal. It's beautiful and repellant at the same time.

The hall gapes before her like another passageway, one from years before.

Her shivering has turned to shaking now. Before her is snow on the ground, a pitted, snowy path.

Before her is a back lane.

This is the dead of night. This is not the time when everything is still and restful, just before dawn. This is the time when things are still moving through the shadows on their nightly wanderings, in the deep dark.

There's a charged energy to this time.

She begins to creep slowly down the hallway, soft electric waves dancing along her skin. There's a strange, faint smell in the air, like something on fire a long way off.

She's at the end of the hallway now and Cody's in the living room.

Cody's sitting on the couch in front of her, and he looks like he has no spirit left in him.

Haven't they been here before? She knows this part.

He's slumped forward heavily onto his chest, legs splayed, hands in his lap, palms upward. Then he raises his head, slow, like a beast pulling itself from muck, and his dark eyes, his eyes so like their mother's, his sad little boy eyes, look right at her.

"Cody," Dawn whispers. "Cody, what's going on?"

She knows that strange things are happening, bad things.

"I've been meaning to tell you," he says.

Dawn reaches out, across the length of the living room—no, just from the other side of the couch. She's sitting beside him now, and she puts her hand against her brother's cheek.

Cody looks at her, urgent and upset. "Tyler and I, we're

doing something…big. Something important. They sent Tyler to me. Do you understand? I can't…Dawn…I don't…"

Dawn can't comprehend what her brother is trying to tell her.

She forgets what he was trying to tell her.

"*YOUR BRO IS beating someone up!*"

Cody and a few others are on a beer run, and Dawn is mechanically lifting a cigarette to her lips, trying to keep warm while she waits for them to come back. The words float toward her on the cold air, and she breathes them in. They sour in the pit of her stomach.

"Beating who up? Where?"

Dawn doesn't like that she sounds so rushed and breathless, so afraid. But she is afraid—Cody fighting is not a good thing. And there's a strange smell, a bite to the air tonight.

Candace looks off to the side before answering, even though there's no one there. She's chewing nervously on a hank of hair, a habit that revolts Dawn. Candace is eighteen or nineteen, ultra-thin and shyly nervous at all times. She's someone's cousin; Dawn can't remember whose. This is the first time Dawn's seen Candace in months. The last time it was summer, and they were sharing a sloppily rolled joint down by the river, tossing sticks into the current to watch them swirl and eddy and be pulled downstream. The boys were off down the bank, having some sort of tree-climbing competition in a giant oak. It was hot and dry, and Dawn and Candace plunked down in the shade, greedily drinking the sugary slush melting at the bottom of their Slurpee cups.

Candace's hair was scraped back in a ponytail and Dawn's eyes lingered on the three teardrop tattoos, homemade blue outlines like rain, that ran from the corner of Candace's eye down to the top of her left cheekbone.

"Do those mean you've killed someone?" Dawn asked brazenly, pointing with her straw.

Candace shut her eyes like the heat had suddenly overwhelmed her, then said, "No. Outlines are for someone you love getting killed," and Dawn didn't say anything, and Candace kept looking out toward the river, and sweat trickled down Dawn's back, and three ghosts hung in the air between them.

Now, in winter, the street light traps Candace and Dawn in its yellow shine, inoculates them against the dark. The dark where Dawn's brother is fighting.

Candace draws a breath and says in a rush, "I don't know! Some guy! They were yelling at each other in the back lane!"

For as long as she lives, Dawn will remember the high-pitched exclamation, of fear or excitement or adrenalin, that punctuated each of Candace's sentences. She'll remember the way, despite her nervous voice, Candace's eyes were half-closed the whole time. Candace in the street light in a short, pink puffer, the ends of her hair sticking to her cheek and her eyelids at half-mast. A photograph in Dawn's mind. She can still feel the way the freezing air contracted, sucked itself across her skin. The way a vacuum opened in the world.

She can still see how, suddenly, Candace's eyes popped wide.

It is Violet's voice that speaks to Dawn from the teen's body.

"Run," Violet tells her, her voice a long wail.

Candace's face and body go momentarily slack before the light returns to her eyes, but Dawn is already running. She jumps the low chain of the parking lot fence and starts down the back lane.

They must be around the bend.

She can't hear anything but her crunching shoes and her breathing.

She rounds the bend.

From this distance, they could be embracing. Two men, boys really, intimately interlocked, their bodies pressed up against the siding of a small detached garage abutting the lane. The garage is a featureless beige, another earth-toned thing in the dullness of that winter night. The snow dirty brown and grey around their feet. A cold and colourless scene, the moon partially hidden by clouds.

She is there, watching.

She stops some ten paces from them and watches what happens.

The cold air rips at her panting throat. There is a panicked buzz in her limbs that she can't seem to direct into action. She just stands there.

Her brother is pressing the other boy up against the vinyl siding of the garage, hard. He's holding him there, leaning into him with the bulk of his body. One of the other boy's arms is up, held uselessly in place by Cody's, the other crushed under him by Cody's weight pushing the boy into the wall.

Cody holds him there.

There is a light just under the roof of the garage, and they move in and out of the small circle it casts. There are specks of bright red blood on the snowy ground, and the snow has been scuffled by their feet in a messy ring. The boy's face, half-illuminated from above, is all angles and deep shadows, and one eye is swollen, like one of her brother's eyes is swollen, like they traded punches in a duel.

Cody's face moves into the meagre light, and she sees that his lip is open and bleeding, too. But her brother is unquestionably winning the fight.

Dawn doesn't know where the knife comes from.

There's a small flurry of movement, and then she catches the glint in Cody's hand. The knife, just a kitchen knife, is in Cody's hand. He holds it awkwardly in an underhand grip and stabs him in the stomach, easily cutting through the boy's sweatshirt but delivering a blow that's shallow and ill-aimed, hitting only flesh on the other boy's side. Though painful, this wound alone, in all likelihood, would not prove fatal. A spasm passes over the face of the other boy. He doesn't scream. Whatever softer sound he might have made, Dawn is too far away to hear.

Cody must have adjusted his grip; his hand swings in an arc and the knife finds muscle in the boy's chest, slides into it.

A short, gargling scream.

Cody stabs a third time, in the chest again. There's something different about this time. There is no autopsy, but this one punctured the boy's right lung, ripping it irreparably.

Cody lets the knife fall to the ground.

He steps back, breathing heavily, and the boy falls, sprawled on his back in the snow.

Just to look away, just to see anything else at all, Dawn looks up at the sky. The clouds hang low, obscuring the moon and the stars.

She looks back at the boy on the ground and sees that it's Jeremy.

And there it is—Dawn's greatest shame, which will settle around her like a cloak for the rest of her life: once she recognized Jeremy, she did not go to him. She remained standing there, struck dumb, numb.

She will always wither inside, attempt to shrivel away from herself, when she thinks about how she did not go and comfort him as he lay there. She knows that people can't predict how they will act in a crisis, how they will react to violence and death—but still, she wonders—always, she wonders: would she have reacted differently, would she have gone to Jeremy, if he'd been someone else? Someone she'd liked more?

The screech of sirens shatters the air. Cop cars come screeching down the lane, red and blue lights pulsing over the blood pooling around the body. The cops get out of their cars and Dawn takes a step forward, and then falls to her knees on the hard ground. She raises her arms above her head, as Cody does, and stares at her brother's back as he's led to the back seat of a cruiser.

Shaking, she hangs her head.

"DAWN, DAWN." Cody's shaking her shoulder. He really wants to tell her something and she's not listening. Can't pay attention.

They're on the blue floral couch, sitting very close together, and one of them has been drinking—no, wait, that's the smell of burning hair, or of an electrical fire. Faint, like a distant sea.

"Cody, I can't hear you," she hears herself say, and she's not inside herself.

She's floating near the ceiling. Her mouth is so dry, and Cody is next to her on the couch.

She's so tired. She's got to go back to bed now.

She's in bed on the ceiling and her throat is scratching.

Her brother is shaking her on the couch.

CHAPTER EIGHTEEN

TYLER

Tyler grew up in a subsidized apartment complex on the eastern edge of town. The town was one of many like it, replicating itself with slight variations across the more northern reaches of the southern provinces. It was small and isolated, and most lives had work at their centre. People livened it up with eating, drinking, camping, and fighting. The downtown was an imperfect square of a few restaurants and bars, and a handful of other businesses: a locally owned grocery store, a thrift store, an insurance broker, a camping supply store chain. Bored teenagers, their thoughts drifting out over the town and away, to elsewhere, sold sleeping bags and

Thermoses to tourists, helped locals fix up their aging gear. The café-cum-bar that served jet-fuel black coffee and omelettes in the mornings, dinner and beer specials in the evenings. It was an insular place, with people that generally preferred being outdoors as much as possible, though they still liked to keep half an eye on what their neighbours were up to.

The natural beauty around the town was a striking contradiction to the industrial heart that drove it. With autumn in the air, the trees looked like they'd been dipped in pots of paint, their canopies turning bright orange and red in wide swaths.

Even farther north, out of view, though their presence was felt for miles, lay the massive wounds of the tar sands. Churned, oily fields and gashes in the earth, metal equipment crawling along the routes, thick smoke billowing into the sky. They looked like pure devastation; like tableaux from the end of the world, from a lightless future. There was little beauty left to be found there, or in the surrounding man camps of workers. Rough places where men released the pressure of their hard, dangerous jobs in different ways—drinking, gambling, lifting the same shitty pair of rusting dumbbells. Uglier ways, too.

Tyler was raised by a single father who did not want to be a father and therefore mostly wasn't. When Tyler was a boy, he was often left alone in their apartment, often for hours. He hated to be alone in the apartment; it felt like waiting in a tomb. There was something hostile about the place. His skin crawled when he was alone inside it.

On summer nights when it was still warm out after dark, he'd play outside, waiting for headlights to illuminate the front of their building, for his father to kill the engine and stagger out.

The prairies rolled out and away from the back of their building. The boy played outside in the glow cast from three security lights affixed to the back of the building at roughly even intervals. The light was yellow-tinged and feeble—it illuminated only a few feet of ground before the imposing, absolute darkness of the prairies beyond took over. How small and inconsequential he felt, waiting for his drunk dad to come home, with most of his neighbours asleep at his back. No matter how hard he strained, or how long he patiently stared, his eyes could not adjust to the darkness. There was nothing to adjust to, no light for his eyes to latch onto. A boy in curdled yellow light, alone on the edge.

One night, Tyler sneaked silently outside and around the back of the building, clutching a flashlight. He was maybe ten years old. His dad had said he'd be home for dinner, but it was after eleven now, and no dad. It was still warm out, and he wore only a light jacket, a nylon shell he didn't even bother to zip up. He breathed the darkness in deeply. He dared himself to walk thirty feet out without the flashlight on. Then, he conceded, he could turn the flashlight on and run back to the apartment building. He would measure the feet by counting slowly, out loud— *onemississippi, twomississippi, threemississippi*—while he walked. He knew he was a coward. He didn't need to hear his dad slur it. He dared himself to do this because he was determined to become braver, more courageous. He was weak in a tough world and *that's a helluva bad combo, kid.*

He shuffled in the patch of light, flicking the flashlight on and off a few times to make sure it would work when he was thirty feet out there in the dark. He didn't want to waste any time letting what courage he had slip away. He clicked the flashlight off and stepped forward, one sneakered foot inching out over the dirt, feeling for the spot where the absence of light began. He took two steps for every *mississippi* that he counted, and by the time he reached fifteen his heart was fluttering. Wings of panic brushed against his ribs. But he kept edging forward in the darkness.

He looked back toward the apartment building—an alien ship, stark and lonely. He turned back to the dark, and that's when he saw the eyes. Flashes of yellow. He could smell a thick, musky, rotting scent. His heart plummeted to his stomach. *Fool,* his dad's voice said in his head.

Standing paralyzed in the darkness, trying to slow his breathing and keep his sight fixed on the dim yellow glow of the cougar's eyes, the boy harboured a secret thought: the cat was waiting for him; it had come for him.

He could hear the animal breathing, maybe ten feet away. The eyes were flashes in the dark. They blinked out and he lost track of them, but then he caught the yellowish gleam again. They didn't seem to be moving any closer. The cougar was sitting there in the dark, watching him. Assessing him. He felt the rhythm of his breath match with the unseen animal's, and they breathed in tandem in the night. The fearful paralysis began to lift off his limbs. He paused, wavering for a moment, and was about to take a step forward, toward the beast, when the sound of a car door slamming shattered their silent communion. He turned instinctively toward the sound, and when he looked back, he couldn't see the eyes anymore. Fear returned tenfold and he bolted back toward the apartment building.

The boy was panting when he reached the door. He caught up to his father as he was trying to fit his key into the lock. His dad saw him and let out a bark of laughter.

"Seen a ghost?"

His dad didn't wait for an answer before stumbling inside, leaving the door hanging open. By the time Tyler had closed and locked the front door and taken off his sneakers and jacket, his dad was passed out on the plaid living room sofa, brown leather cowboy boots still on his feet. His dad worked in administration for one of the companies working the tar sands. Even as a boy, Tyler heard talk about the man camps. He often wondered if his father went there on some of his nights out. The nights when he came home wasted, as usual, but also reeking of something else. Under the anger, the extra drunken bluster, there was shame. Tyler watched his dad sleep on the sofa, oblivious in his deep unconsciousness, and imagined opening the front door and beckoning to the creature in the night.

He never told his father about the cougar. The next morning it was raining when he woke up, any hope of finding paw prints washed away by noon. His dad slept well into the afternoon and woke in a foul mood, banging around the kitchen making coffee, snapping at the boy to keep out of his way.

As Tyler got older, he clashed with his father more and more. Pointless, ridiculous arguments when Tyler started coming home drunk, too. They got physical a few times during his teens and early adulthood, until the night Tyler hit his dad so hard the man, now in his seventies, fell to the kitchen linoleum, the thin skin of his cheekbone split and oozing blood. Tyler tried to apologize, to help his dad up, but the old man brushed him off, rose shakily, got his jacket and car keys, and took off.

Later, Tyler wouldn't remember what they'd been fighting about. When he opened the front door to three police officers on the step, the blue and red lights of their cruisers flashing in his eyes, he knew instantly, in some deep part of himself, what had happened.

"The accident occurred on the highway, on the way back from the oil fields. Your dad have any reason to be out there this time of night?"

Tyler appraised the female deputy. She'd arrested his dad for drunk and disorderlies before, as had most of the officers on the force. *The fucking old fool. The drunk old fuck.*

"No," Tyler said, meeting her eyes, "not that I know of."

One of the other cops stepped forward and put a heavy hand on his shoulder. "We're awfully sorry for your loss, son. We can tell you that it does, uh, look like, uh…right now, it does look as though…"

"Your father was driving while intoxicated when

the accident occurred," the woman cop said over the sputtering of her co-worker.

Tyler appreciated her directness. "Thanks for letting me know," he said, and met her eyes again.

He was twenty-one that night, the night his father died, and he was twenty-two when he married Marie, the cop at his door.

TALL AND SHAGGY BLOND, with broad shoulders and darting, calculating eyes at twenty-nine, Tyler loped down the sidewalk like he didn't want to seem like he was in a hurry. It was a sleepy, drizzling Sunday afternoon and the town was quiet.

Tyler was walking away from a nondescript one-and-a-half split-level. The curtains were drawn at this house. This house had a stillness more profound than the stillness of the day around it. The house he'd lived in with his wife, Marie, for almost six years.

Tyler never wanted the house. They were living in the slightly damp but roomy basement of an older woman who needed the rental income, where they'd been living since getting married, and Tyler didn't see why they needed anything more than that. But Marie's dad saw things differently, as he tended to do. He was a bullish man, shorter than Tyler but infinitely more self-assured and intimidating. He insisted on buying them the house because he didn't think his precious only daughter should be living in a basement as a married woman. He didn't think Tyler was taking proper care of his daughter, and he didn't like that everyone could see it.

So they moved into the house. On the day they took possession, Tyler stood silently and smiled, thanked the man whose sweaty hand pumped his own as he said, "Gotta show you the way somehow, eh, boy?"

From the second they moved in, the house felt too close, tight like a trap. He never felt comfortable, could never truly settle in. Marie decorated the place with her father's money and tried to draw Tyler into hours roaming the aisles of Home Depot as she asked for his grunted opinion on paint swatches and wallpaper patterns. Marie was only a cop for a year before becoming a secretary for her father's development business. She'd hated the job, hated the jeers and stares of her mostly male co-workers ("Can't blame 'em, can you?" Tyler had said, trying to make light of it, but she'd turned away, lips turned down). She'd quit as overdose deaths were starting to climb because she didn't want to have to keep telling the despairing and disbelieving parents of people she'd grown up with, gone to high school with, that their kid had died. She was now racing toward stay-at-home-mom status, and Tyler didn't know how to put on the brakes.

Marie wasn't meant to be such a big part of the story for Tyler, not really. She was a side character who somehow conned her way into a leading-woman role. She was irritating, constantly questioning him, asking him to explain himself, his activities. At first, she'd picked at him with a smile and insisted that it was not picking at all, that she was just asking him innocent questions about his day, his work, his life. His skin pricked and itched when he was around her, and he entertained the idea that he may have developed an allergy to her. It was little wonder he lost his temper with her sometimes, the way she made him feel.

"Why are you so angry with me all the time?" Marie blurted out one night, quick and low. She didn't meet his eyes.

"You haven't seen angry," he paused to sneer at her on his way to the back of the house, to the messy, only semi-insulated sunroom he claimed as his own. He felt a thrill of satisfaction at seeing her scared face.

Tyler liked to hang out in the back room—work out, listen to music, tinker with woodwork. He also liked to think while he was there. Long and deep, about his life and the people in it.

Marie and her arrogant little father. Their main purpose in life was to humiliate him, to debase him to something lower than ... dirt. Lower than the dirt he'd played in as a child on the outskirts of this dismal town, where he still sometimes drove to sit and drink beer—usually after Marie had pushed him too far again and made him slap or shove her. He hoped to see a muscled, tawny creature come into his headlights. Come to lead him away.

The cougar never came for him again, but someone did.

Tyler approached the end of the street and took a left, down a sloping road dotted with houses. He'd parked his car there earlier, when he got home, so it would look like he'd been away from home all day to any neighbours sticking their noses where they didn't belong. Marie's voice had been shrilly ringing in his ears—"We need to talk. Now." She'd called him at work and demanded he come home. One of her nosy bitch friends had called her, again, but she wouldn't tell him what she'd been told. He tried to think back to who'd been at the bar the other night, the last time he'd been in and gotten particularly rowdy. What dim corner he'd been spotted in, and with whom. How dare she tell him they needed to talk? Was she thinking she'd leave him? He'd almost guffawed at the thought as he'd entered the house to find Marie standing rigidly in the kitchen, arms crossed over her chest, face set.

As he hurried away, he didn't look back at his still home. In the decades he would continue to live, as himself, and then as something else, he would rarely think about that hated house, or about Marie. On the tenth anniversary of this day, he would think back for the first time, spurred by the particular way light fell across linoleum, to how he'd left her, on their kitchen floor. It was like looking at a picture in a book, one he hadn't read. The image meant nothing to him. He let that unearthed memory go and never thought of his wife again.

He wasn't sure what his plan was. He didn't think that far. Didn't really think at all, actually, not in the moment. He just drove south.

He wound up at a gas station diner eventually. One of those big complexes off the side of a highway that glowed an ambivalent welcome. Some people who ended up here rested, some hid, others prowled.

The diner was neon lit and low-slung, with sloping curves, a leftover flight of architectural fancy. Inside, the booths were wide and deep, covered with burst veins of cracked vinyl. There were Formica tabletops and a line of swivelling metal stools at the bar. Fluorescent lighting hummed in its tubing. Everyone here was just passing through, just stopping by, except for the few farmers with properties nearby who come in every day for coffee and, sometimes, a full greasy breakfast. But even they didn't talk to each other. The code was silence.

It was nighttime, past dinner—late enough for only a handful of long-haul truckers to be scattered across the dining room. Tyler sat close to one of the large windows overlooking the wide asphalt expanse of the parking lot. Beyond the parking lot, the lanes of the highway; beyond that, fields and farms and sky.

Tyler's eyes passed over the menu again and again, skittering sightless over the laminated words. He was keenly aware that the entire police department would now be mobilized to find him, Marie's father roaring behind them to quicken their steps.

He'd hit five different ATMs in five different towns along the way, so he'd hopefully have enough cash to not leave a trail. He'd been staying in cheap motels for three nights now. He didn't like the anonymous motels. The thin, scratchy covers on the beds irritated his skin and nothing felt clean.

He took jerky little sips from the white mug of black coffee in front of him and watched the headlights that swung occasionally into the parking lot. Bugs skittered over and collided with the window, drawn by the light inside. He rapped a knuckle on the glass, but none of the bugs reacted.

A love song played on the radio, a pop song with flutes in the chorus. He sipped his coffee and considered how much farther he could drive tonight. He was confident he could make it to the next town with another refill of this strong coffee. He turned to signal for the waitress and saw that a man had come through the front door. He didn't know why his eyes stopped to rest on the stranger, but they did.

He was on the shorter side and clearly well-muscled, even beneath his jacket. The hem of his jeans were frayed and muddy. He was wearing workboots and had a furrowed, intense brow. He looked like ten thousand other men Tyler had seen in his life, but something about him resonated with a low but compelling frequency, like he was gently vibrating. Humming. Tyler stared at him, And the man's eyes landed on Tyler. He raised an arm in greeting and Tyler instinctively raised his eagerly back, then regretted it, feeling foolish.

The man slid into the booth across from him.

Tyler was suddenly deeply uneasy. "Who are you?" he asked, keeping his voice low in case the answer was something he didn't want to hear.

The man smiled and motioned for the waitress.

"A friend," he said and ordered a cup of coffee and a strawberry waffle. The strawberry waffle made Tyler relax a bit, so he asked for a refill on his coffee.

Once the waitress had left again, cigarette between her fingers before she was even out the door for her break, the man extended his hand across the tabletop and said, "Micah. We've been watching you."

Tyler hesitated, wary again, before he grabbed the man's dry, callused hand. "Tyler," he said.

Micah nodded and said, "We know." And then he started to talk.

Micah said some unbelievable shit. It was truly unbelievable what he said this group could do for Tyler, what they could make him into, what power they could show him.

Tyler felt the buzz, the hum, again.

Any way out, any possible way out.

Tyler looked across the parking lot as Micah talked between bites of his waffle. The bugs banged their hard bodies in a symphony against the glass. Headlights swept the black asphalt, weary travellers turning toward the neon.

Other things travelled along these prairie highways; other things moved under cover of night.

Tyler stared out at the constant motion, the continuous movement through the night, and he didn't think about Marie, or the remnants of the life he'd left behind. He thought about the possibility of moving forward, toward something new and unknown.

He stared out the window and the distant pinpoint of high beams on the road looked like a cat's eyes in the dark.

CHAPTER NINETEEN

A crackling licks over her skin and jerks Dawn back to the present.

She's standing at the end of the hallway and the front door is swinging open, the cold night air rushing in. There is a small pile of snow on the welcome mat, drifting inwards. The pull in her navel tells her she has to go—she has to follow.

She yanks open the hall closet and grabs her father's parka, the first one her hand closes on, zipping it up over her pyjamas. She grabs a black toque and scarf from the sagging cardboard box of winter accessories and heads toward the gently swinging front door.

She winds the scarf around her face and pulls the toque low over her ears. Her legs are freezing, the wind whipping through her thin pyjama pants. At least the parka hangs to just below her knees, protecting her thighs from the worst of the wind.

There's an urgent crackle in the air all around her.

She shoves her hands deep in the pockets and heads for the street, following the insistent hook in her navel.

She stops when she reaches the curb marking the end of their front lawn and looks both ways along the street. One end opens onto the road that bisects the entire neighbour-hood, the one way in off the city's arterial highway, and the way back out again at either the eastern or western limit. Back into the city or out into the open prairies.

The other end of the street curves and, after a few more blocks, opens up into the new development where Crystal and Jake Reed live in their carefully partitioned spaces.

Something is standing in the wintry shadows at the curved end of the street.

Dawn's breath is sour in her tight throat.

The hare stands in the soft moonlight.

It stands on its hind legs, front paws dangling. She can't see its face from this far away, but she's sure it's looking at her. There's a coldness deep within her. Its coarse fur quivers over musculature far too large for a rabbit. It terrifies her in a primordial way, on a level beyond her comprehension.

The hare tilts its head questioningly at Dawn, and she realizes this is what she's meant to follow. As she walks toward it, the hare drops to all fours and runs.

It doesn't hop like a rabbit; it runs like a stalking cat.

Dawn feels the cry as it exits her throat. She is trembling so hard her teeth clack together. She leans over, puts her elbows on her knees, and fights the wave of nausea at the *wrongness* of it. She's seen something humans aren't meant to see.

Dawn straightens up with effort. The thing is gone from view around the bend. Something is grinding in a distant place, some machine droning on.

She has to walk.

She holds her breath as she rounds the bend. The hare is at the far end, on the left branch of the street. The one heading toward the Reeds' house. Dawn puts her head down and marches in that direction. They wind their way through the streets—rabbit and woman, moving toward the great disturbance in this strange night.

They are heading for the fields.

The Reeds' house is entirely dark, and both Crystal's compact Honda and Jake's huge 4x4 are gone from the driveway. The hare is at the dead end of the street. The light from the new development doesn't extend far into the barren field on the other side. Beyond is blackness dark as the sea. The hare turns and vanishes into the night. The fear that grips Dawn's heart threatens to choke her. The thought of being alone out on the dark, frozen, wind-swept prairie is harrowing.

The wind howls.

Over the low, dangerously spiked stumps of bare bushes, across the hard ridges of the frozen ground, between the copses of trees that dot the landscape—the wind howls.

It takes the breath from Dawn's lungs, and she walks with her arms out in front of her, trying to form a pocket of protection for her face.

She presses forward, peering into the distance for the rabbit, a blur in the darkness ahead. Dawn stumbles after it, hoping she won't catch a clumsy boot on a stump and fall, breaking an ankle, a wrist. Smashing her face on the hard ground and getting stuck out here, slowly freezing to death. Her mind flashes back to Jeremy's smashed face. Her breath hitches, and then she lets it go—she howls with the wind. She lets out a scream, ragged and wretched, that is carried off as soon as it escapes her mouth.

DAWN IS FIVE YEARS OLD and it's the middle of summer, the air thick and cloying with the sweet smell of cut grass starting to rot, the earthy scent of vegetation so ripe and lush it cannot be contained. All life glories in the fullness of itself. The sun beams and bakes, and it's enough to lie in the shade of a solid tree and feel the weight and movement of her body as it breathes in the summer air. Dawn wants to swallow this moment, this day, and keep it in her belly, there for her to access whenever she wants.

It's the weekend, and Martin and Violet, in a rare mood to do something as a family, have piled the kids into the car and driven dirt and gravel paths out to a field deemed perfect for a picnic. Martin lugs a plastic cooler out of the back seat, and Violet lays a blanket on the grass. There are cheese and butter sandwiches and apple slices covered in lemon juice and cinnamon (a Violet special). Violet and Martin sit on opposite ends of the blanket, heads tilted back to accept the sun on their faces, and Cody and Dawn go sprinting free around the field. They've chosen it randomly and there are no signs posted. It may be a farmer's rarely visited back acreage; in any case, there is no one else here, no one to tell them to get out. When they're done running and exploring, the kids come back to their parents on the blanket and devour the food—sun-warmth and good flavours and a feeling like togetherness, like belonging, all mingling into something soft and safe.

Dawn holds this summer day close to her heart. It is one of the few times her parents are completely relaxed and content, free of that mysterious and never-mentioned spectre that hangs over them daily, otherwise. That spectre that touches them both but hugs Violet tightest. That prevents her from revelling in the ease and comfort of a tenderly held hug, and that makes her feel other things far too much. Some things she just can't shake off. But here, where there's no one, where the sky is domed and endless and the air is hot and still—here, in this moment, Violet sets everything down for a bit. She closes her eyes and drifts with the breeze.

Dawn eats her sandwich and looks over at her mother—at ease, eyes shut like she's having a nice dream, her hands relaxed in her lap, her skin lovely and glowing a golden copper in the sun. This is the Violet that Dawn wants to keep close: the woman her mother could be. The woman her mother is. Just like she's the woman who drifts off into her own mind for weeks at a time, who floats beyond the grasp of her husband and her children. But Dawn wishes this was the woman her mother could be most often, the part of herself that is closest to the surface, that touches others and allows others to touch her.

Dawn finishes her sandwich and scrunches the blanket between her bare toes, burying her face in her knees and smiling into the secret cave she's created with her body.

She wants to stay like this forever.

THE MEMORY OF the summer prairie fades back to the frigid field in front of her. Dawn loses all sense of time and distance out on the open plains. She has no idea how long she's been walking or how far she is from home when the wind begins, nearly imperceptibly at first, to quiet. As she inches forward over the next few feet of frozen ground, the wind dies down around her. In front of her is a copse of trees, sparse and stark, with bare dead branches. Between the trunks she can make out a clearing that the trees encircle.

Along the inside edge of the clearing, several vehicles are parked. Dawn's shins feel hard and frozen, her face numb. The metallic red of Jake's 4x4 glints dully. Beside it, Crystal's car.

As she looks at the familiar cars parked out here on the strange, dark prairie, there's a disorienting shift in her perception.

And she realizes she had it wrong all along.

Terrible things happen side by side with the ordinary.

The air crackles around her.

Dawn crouches and steps quietly forward.

CHAPTER TWENTY

The clearing is almost a perfect circle, the size of a large swimming pool, guarded by trees. Near the far end, Jake and Crystal and Tyler and Cody are standing in a semicircle with their backs to Dawn.

In front of them, a portal.

Like the hole she saw open in the living room, there is a roughly circular void, a ripping-open of the atmosphere, suspended several feet above the ground. A black so black it's like looking at nothing, at antimatter.

The innards move.

A constant, sinuous motion. Like sinuous snakes, their scales shifting over their bodies, their bodies shifting over one another, endlessly eating themselves and each other.

Dawn places a hand on the truck to steady herself against intense vertigo. The portal is big, several times the size of the one opened in the living room. And it's tilted at an angle so that it doesn't quite lie parallel to the earth. It is an inviting angle, an angle that says: *Come to me*.

From deep within the pit, and simultaneously from deep within her bones, emanates a resonant and grinding sound.

Dawn hardly dares to breathe.

She takes a few steps back in the snow, crouching even lower beside the truck, compelled to move away from the hole in the air and its crackling energy like she's shielding herself from a brightly burning sun. She shudders from the thought of what infernal reckoning could come from that void. The air bites at and dries out her lungs. She makes herself look back toward the gathering.

The four figures appear to be just standing there, staring at the hole. Jake is in the middle of the semicircle, with Crystal and Tyler to his left, and Cody to his right. They're all dressed like they left in a hurry. Crystal's wearing her parka but no toque, and sneakers on her feet. Cody's wearing a thick plaid of Martin's, layered over a hoodie. Jake's wearing a brown leather bomber over a hoodie, jeans, and workboots. And he's holding something. Dawn squints to make it out—a small book. No, a piece of paper.

Malice hangs in the air, like it's attached to the strange, translucent sheets of pale light that still shimmer in the atmosphere. The buzzing intensifies, but now, under it, Dawn can make out another noise.

Jake's voice, chanting.

He's speaking in a language she doesn't know. She strains to hear better. It sounds like the same few words over and over again, and as the buzzing intensifies further, Jake's voice crescendoes, until it's booming out over the clearing, reverberating, echoing like they're in an amphitheatre. Dawn brings her hands to her ears. His voice penetrates to the very marrow of her bones, shaking them, shaking her from the inside out. She clings to the truck to keep from falling over into the snow.

The movement within the portal becomes more rapid, and layered, like it reaches deep, deep down. Dawn has to look away. When she looks at the swirling mass, she feels like her whole being is falling forward through space toward the hole, like the distance will accordion like elastic and she'll be pitched into the void, calling to her.

The grinding, buzzing machinations have turned into something else, into a thrashing sound. An angry, rageful sound.

Dawn wants to look away, but she does not.

The portal grinds and buzzes and the movement becomes frantic and there's a pressure building in Dawn's head like an earth-shattering wave is about to crest, the peak is about to be reached, and *something* is about to burst forth into the world.

And then, so suddenly it takes a few seconds to register, everything stops.

Tyler has his hands in his hair. Cody is looking intently at Jake, searching his face for an answer. Jake is looking at the hole, at the paper crumpled in his hand, and then back at the hole. Crystal appears to be on the verge of tears, her face slipping toward a meltdown.

Jake, Tyler, and Cody are talking close together now, stealing worried glances at the hole and making short, quick gestures. Tyler is chewing on the side of his thumb. Crystal is crying and pacing back and forth behind the men. Whatever was meant to happen, clearly, has not.

The void is now motionless, and nothing has ever looked more dead, more bereft of life. Dawn feels a terrible, unnameable longing. The air, she realizes, is back to normal, and the only sound is the low wind.

She slaps herself across the face. Dawn needs to move. Closer to where the hole is, to avoid the others when they come back to their vehicles. She doesn't want to think about them catching her out here. She glances back across the clearing to make sure they aren't halfway to her already, but they've moved closer to the void.

As she creeps from tree to tree along the northern side of the oval clearing, trying to angle herself so she stays hidden, she prays they'll be too distracted to see her. *Please let them go soon and not see me. Let them go soon and not see me,* she repeats in her head over and over like an incantation.

She stops behind a tree that should be big enough to hide her completely and leans over to rub at her frozen shins, hoping to bring some feeling back to them. She tries to tuck the ends of her pyjama pants further into her boots. It's so cold.

Please let them go soon and not see me.

She peers around the trunk of the tree.

Cody and Tyler are very near the void, both turning from it to look back at Jake and Crystal, who are arguing intensely, inches from each other's faces. Their voices are loud and angry, but the wind carries their words away.

And the roiling within the hole starts again.

It speeds up rapidly, wildly, a million snakes entwined and writhing, but the movement seems different now, somehow disturbed.

Crystal isn't crying anymore, but her cheeks are a mess with tears, mascara, and snot. She is beyond caring, her hair sticking up wildly. Jake looks much more composed than his wife, though he also seems to be working hard to stifle a growing panic. Disguising it with rage. Dawn reads the contempt etched on his face as he looks at Crystal, and she doesn't wonder why a woman whose husband looks at her like that would still be with him.

She knows there are a hundred little whys that have all added up to this moment.

Because Crystal and Jake were born in the same place and grew up together. Because they met when they were young, and it's romantic and wholesome to marry someone you've known your entire life. Because Crystal got pregnant a year into dating, her first year of the nursing program she'd finally committed to, and just like her mother, she wouldn't even hear the word *abortion*. Because the baby turned out to be twins, and Jake was delighted, and Crystal was so, so tired, navigating the care of two helpless newborns alone while Jake slept in the other room so he wouldn't be too tired for work in the morning. Because Crystal got pregnant again after that—"So soon!" her friends chirped, laughing, and Crystal laughed with them and decided not to tell them that Jake didn't allow her to use birth control. Because when she had a miscarriage, he held her and told her he loved her in a voice low and soothing. And because he still opened doors for her when they went on date nights to dinner and a movie, and when he insisted they had to keep trying for more kids, she reminded herself that this is love, that they are in love. Because her mother loves him, maybe more than she loves Crystal, and would be furious if Crystal ruined such a good thing. Because Jake started dropping hints, subtle at first, and then less so, that certain things Crystal did, like going out for drinks with friends, maybe caused the miscarriage, so she stopped going out with her friends as much, and then at all. Because she told herself this was fine, that a man like Jake will make demands, and those demands should be met, because ultimately, surely, he knows best. Because if he doesn't know best, then this life doesn't make sense, her life doesn't make sense.

Because she saw a meanness, a coldness in him that was in herself, too.

Dawn watches Jake's face. The hardness and the hatred she'd seen a flash of in their basement blazes forth. His face is red, and his eyes are sharp and hateful. Crystal retreats and cowers, bending away from Jake. In the fear on her face, Dawn can read all the other times this has happened.

But this time is different.

It happens so fast.

Jake bears down on the much smaller form of his wife. He grabs Crystal. She's grown so thin over the past few months that his thick hand encircles her upper arm. He drags her across a few feet of snowy ground. She shrieks, clawing at him, but he drags her a few more feet.

And then he stops and throws her the final, short distance.

Jake throws Crystal into the void.

Time stops. There's an intense smell, like a chemical fire and the briny salt of the sea.

Suspended, Crystal makes a strangled gurgling noise from the depths of her throat, a sound Dawn has never heard a person make before.

Time starts again. There's a great hiss, an electric *sizzling*, and Crystal's body connects with the black surface of the portal and immediately vanishes.

She disappears completely.

There's silence in the clearing, or perhaps it's just that Dawn hears nothing. That her ears and mind block it all out. In the next instant, the wind comes back and she hears a voice calling out. For a wild second she thinks it's Crystal, that she's somewhere just out of sight, maybe hurt, but they could still pull her back. Then Dawn registers that it's a man's voice.

Jake is shouting from near the lip of the hole. Tyler has one hand around the back of the other man's neck, like he's palming a basketball, and has hoisted him unnaturally high into the air with apparent ease.

Jake dangles, his whole large body limp, seemingly unable to struggle or fight, only to cry out in panicked terror, his eyes roving around, searching to connect with who, Dawn doesn't know.

Dawn wants to see Jake suffer.

Her heart doesn't even flutter when Tyler releases his impossible grip and Jake's body meets the blackness and vanishes.

An annihilation.

A terrible hissing sound, a satisfied smile on Tyler's face, an electric crackle in the air.

Tyler walks over to Cody, who stands oddly slack now, and she catches the word *liability* as Tyler puts a hand on his shoulder. Her brother is standing very still. Tyler speaks to Cody nearly nose to nose, hands on either side of his head, punctuating his words with slight shakes for emphasis. Cody nods along, placid and vacant.

She has no idea what she's just seen, what she's still seeing, but she knows that Tyler is something other than a man, or he is a man corrupted, and Dawn needs to get him—whatever the fuck he is—away from her brother. She scans the ground for a weapon. Tossing aside a stumpy, useless twig, she spies a solid branch beneath a tree ahead. It's closer to Tyler, Cody, and the hole, directly in Tyler's sightline. She feels her smallness acutely, unprepared and alone in the cold, with dangerous men. But what else can she do? She goes for the branch.

When she straightens up with it, Tyler and Cody are standing side by side, five feet away, staring directly at her.

Her breath catches in her throat. They move toward her, and she steps back involuntarily.

Cody's movements exactly mirror and directly follow Tyler's, a fraction of a second later, like Tyler is the puppet master and Cody is tied to him with strings. They march in lockstep and cover the short distance quickly, stopping a foot from where she stands. There's no point trying to run over the uneven snow and ice into the open, frigid prairie. There are no houses or farms anywhere on the horizon no matter which direction she turns. She's already lost.

Dawn swings the branch out in front of her like she's warding off a pack of stray dogs.

Tyler barks out a laugh. "Come on now, Dawn. There's no need for that."

"What the hell are you?"

Her brother's eyes are glassy and glazed, slack like his body, which looks even stranger up close, like all his muscles are limp, but an unseen force is holding him firmly upright. He doesn't look like her brother. He looks like an empty shell of a man, hollowed of his spirit.

Tyler's smile widens and his face flickers, like a glitch in the software, a small hop through time. "That's neither here nor there."

"It seems pretty fuckin' relevant!"

He laughs, genuine this time, and shakes his head. And then he pauses and his eyes seem to lose focus, like a daydreamer's or someone caught in a memory, and then he refocuses and looks at her.

"You know what? Fuck it. I like you. I'll let you live."

Tyler shrugs, like it's a casual decision, like he's saying yes to a second helping of a particularly delicious dinner, and then he turns and walks away, and her brother turns and walks away with him.

Toward the hole.

"Wait!" she calls out, but they don't.

Then she's running toward them, toward the terrible void, and she's calling out again, her voice whipped away by the wind. Tyler and Cody reach the lip of the portal just as she clears the edge of the trees, and the wind screams in the openness of the clearing, but she keeps going.

Tyler's hands are moving, he's mumbling something, and the hole seems to rise, to tilt upwards, so that it becomes more like a doorway. The blackness within begins to glisten and gleam, and then it parts, slithering backwards over itself to reveal a passageway.

Dawn stops a few feet away, close enough that she could almost touch them. The passageway flickers, and it's a dark corridor. It flickers again, and it's a back lane on a winter night. Flickers and it's a dark corridor. Flickers and it's a back lane dotted with what look like red flowers but she soon realizes are huge paw prints, pressed into the snow in blood.

Tyler and her brother stand in front of the doorway. Tears leak from the corners of Dawn's eyes and freeze across her cheeks. They both turn to look at her, and Tyler smiles, a false smile with no warmth. Cody smiles, too, but it's not her brother's smile. His real smile, the exact contours of it and how his face and eyes danced, she'll remember for the rest of her life.

Tyler and Cody turn away and step over the bottom lip of the portal, and as they walk down the passageway, the hole swallows them in darkness, closing behind them, folding in on itself, pulling its outer edges into the centre like something being sucked quickly down a drain, so that in a few seconds, in the blink of an eye, the two men, and the hole, are gone.

Dawn is standing alone in a clearing in the freezing winter, crying.

Her whole being wants to collapse to the ground, to press her face into the snow and lie there until the cold takes her. She feels emptied out. She'd rather be dead than be this cold and alone. Her bones are cold. She falls to her knees and she doesn't feel anything. The skin of her legs has gone numb, frozen, and she can't feel the snow and ice biting into her flesh. The numbness burns. She wants to tip forward and lie down forever.

As she's about to give in, still on her knees, she catches movement in the corner of her eye, in the trees. Her mother, shimmering and translucent, shifting in and out of focus in the atmosphere, comes toward her.

Violet is nearly colourless, like a faded photograph that's been left in the sun. But her hair is long and beautiful, and her eyes are urgent but soft. Her hands don't shake, like they often did in life. Dawn stares, unable to form any words, and as she stares at her mother, she hopes for the first time not that Violet will return but that Violet is free now, no longer trapped by the heaviness of who she was when she was alive, and of all the things that happened to her. Dawn won't ever know what those things were. Some silences will never be broken. But perhaps she doesn't need to know. There are other parts of her mother, even gone, that Dawn can still come to know.

Dawn reaches out her hand to her mother.

Violet raises her hand. Her arm is insubstantial, made of air or electricity or some other invisible force.

Inside Dawn, something begins to thaw.

Violet flickers and is gone.

CHAPTER TWENTY-ONE

awn struggles to her feet. She's so stiff with cold she can only move slowly. She lowers her head against the wind, gritting her teeth. Her joints hurt, but she forces herself forward. She covers ground slowly but steadily, heading straight for Jake's truck.

She says a quick, silent prayer, peers in through the window, and—"Yes!" She lets out a ragged shout of triumph. Like a good old country boy, Jake left his keys on the passenger seat and the truck unlocked. She claws open the driver's door and climbs in.

In the surge of adrenalin, she almost doesn't hear it. A quiet voice. She breaks out in a sweat underneath her parka, and for a horrible second, she imagines she will look behind her and find the hare. She forces herself to back out of the truck and listen. A small voice, definitely. A child's voice, calling for help.

She sucks in a breath and her eyes fall on Crystal's Honda. She jogs over as quickly as her body will allow and peers in the window. She sees them. Crystal and Jake's little boys are huddled together in the centre of the back seat, clutching each other desperately. They stare at her with tear-stained faces. She yanks on the door handle, it opens and she crouches down and looks at them.

"You're okay, don't worry, you're okay now. I'm going to take us somewhere safe, okay?" She speaks in a reassuring stream as she scans the front seats and, yes, Crystal's keys are there, too.

"I'm going to get in the car now, okay? I'm going to get in the front seat and drive us away now, somewhere safe."

The only thing she can think to do is keep talking. The cold engine sputters, and she fears she'll have to herd the mute boys over to the truck instead, but it catches and starts. She turns the heat all the way up and twists in her seat to look at them.

"Here we go, okay?"

They say nothing.

The car rocks and rolls over the lumpy ground, and Dawn prays silently that she's heading in the right direction. She keeps glancing back at the small, drawn faces in the rear-view mirror. As she drives, the sun slowly crests the horizon, at first a barely perceptible lightening of the sky. Her numb, burning hands struggle to grip the wheel, but she pushes aside the cries of her body to feed and hydrate it and let it sleep. She turns the radio on to keep alert and glances at the boys again, but they register no reaction. She tries to avoid the low shrubs and deep ruts.

After about fifteen minutes, she sees the hazy outline of the city's downtown rise in the near distance. *Holy fuck, we made it.* She drives as fast as she dares toward the glorious sight, revving the car's engine as it protests. After a few more minutes of off-roading, they reach the edge of the new development, near where the Reeds' street dead-ends, exactly where Dawn first followed the hare out into the fields.

The car grinds over the curb and settles with a jolt onto the street. She looks at the fields behind them now. *What did the boys see in the clearing?* The queasiness in her stomach threatens to turn to bile in her throat as she recalls Jake's rough hand grabbing Crystal's hair. Cody's vacant eyes before he turned from her and was walked away. She shakes her head to clear it and concentrates on the road in front of her.

Dawn guides the car through the silent early-morning streets. Most people are still sleeping, hunkered down in their homes. It's going to be a bright day, the rising sun bringing its cold, clear light, offering illumination but little warmth. They pass an elderly woman with a fuzz of white hair, jogging laboriously down the side of the road. She raises a hand in greeting and Dawn automatically does, too, watching her pass by like an alien vision. The daily movements of life seem even farther from her now than ever before. She swallows the bile down hard.

As she turns the car toward Mrs. Cleary's street, apprehension and shame and guilt bubble over in her. What is she going to tell her? She doesn't even know what she saw, has no way of explaining it. With a stabbing pain in her chest, she realizes Mrs. Cleary will probably think she had something to do with whatever happened, maybe even that she killed Jake and Crystal.

And Tyler and Cody? Are they dead, too? she wonders. A feeling in her gut, the way the portal parted for them, tells her they aren't.

She looks worriedly back at the two small boys in the back seat, silently looking out the window. "Almost there," she says.

She pulls into Mrs. Cleary's driveway. The boys scramble out before she's even turned off the engine.

The front door is flung wide and Mrs. Cleary kneels in the entryway with both boys pressed to her chest, face buried in the tops of their heads. She looks up and sees Dawn approaching and stands up, a boy wrapped around each leg. She's wearing a pink and white jersey nightgown and slippers, her face creased and puffy, her eyes bloodshot.

Dawn stands on the front step unsure what to do. As her mind races, Mrs. Cleary says, "Come in," before reaching out and pulling Dawn through the door.

The front hallway is dim compared to the brightness outside. Dawn stops to allow her eyes to adjust. Mrs. Cleary sweeps the boys down the hall to the kitchen, snatching off their winter gear and dropping it to the floor as they go, saying, "We'll get you warmed up, get you some hot chocolate. Come. Come, now."

After a moment's hesitation, Dawn removes her boots and follows them down the hall. Her body and mind protest every movement, wailing for sleep and stillness. When she enters the kitchen, Mrs. Cleary gives her a glass of water and Dawn has to choke back a sob she's so unbelievably grateful. She takes the glass in shaky hands and gulps the water down. Mrs. Cleary looks her up and down and says, "I'll get you some juice, too," then turns to the boys. "Into the living room, you two! You can put your show on. Cuddle up under the afghans," she says and ushers them out of the room before busying herself making hot chocolate.

Mrs. Cleary's movements are tense. There's a rip in her nightgown along her right shoulder where the seam has burst. Dawn can't remember ever seeing Mrs. Cleary in such a state of dishevelment. She looks like a stranger in her own neat kitchen. Mrs. Cleary carries two mugs to the boys, and Dawn can hear the theme song of a popular cartoon about a talking donkey that is also a firefighter. Mrs. Cleary brings a glass of orange juice to the kitchen table.

Dawn sits down across from her and, after a few gulps of juice, meets her eyes.

Mrs. Cleary assesses Dawn coolly over the rim of her mug of hot chocolate. Dawn's insides squirm under her gaze. She recalls vividly what Mrs. Clearly was like when Dawn was young—a semi-forbidding, semi-comforting presence, like she could take on the world and win, but she could also direct that iron will against you if she chose. Her eyes are a pale, pale blue, like a diluted watercolour of the sky, cinched with a web of crow's feet.

Mrs. Cleary finally speaks. "You weren't supposed to be here."

She folds her hands in front of her on the table. "It threw something off. Your energy... your brother... I don't know."

Mrs. Cleary turns and gazes out the kitchen window, like she's looking for an answer. The noises of the day are beginning in earnest now: people moving around in their homes and driving places, animals and insects rustling in the brush. A portly, brown squirrel clings to the bark halfway down a tree trunk, its head raised and pointed keenly, listening.

Dawn stares mutely at the woman, understanding battling revulsion as Mrs. Cleary turns back to face her.

"No doubt Crystal did something wrong." Mrs. Cleary sighs with disappointment, like they're having any old conversation.

"Don't you care that she's dead?" Dawn blurts out.

Mrs. Cleary stares down at her hands, clasped in front of her on the sunflower-patterned tablecloth. When she looks up again, she is not crying.

Her pale eyes look through Dawn. "I care that the opening didn't work," she says.

Dawn cannot stay in this house any longer. Her whole being is shrieking in protest.

She pushes her chair back and stumbles out of the kitchen and toward the front door. Her bleary mind half-expects Mrs. Cleary to pursue her, to stop her from leaving, maybe even to attack her. She can almost feel the hand grasping her shoulder. But it doesn't come, and Dawn moves quickly through the living room where the boys are watching TV, not looking at them—she can't look at them—and reaches the door.

The cold outside is a shock all over again. Dawn pushes forward into the wind anyway. She trudges home, head bowed, thinking only of warmth and rest. She leaves her clothes in a heap beside her bed, crawls under the covers, and is instantly taken by sleep.

SHE'S SCREAMING AND *screaming at Crystal. She knows she's in another room, even though she can't see her. She's screaming for her to respond, but she doesn't.*

Then she's sitting beside her brother on the front step of their house, in the sunshine, and they aren't speaking, but it feels like they just were, and the silence is comfortable and comforting, and for as long as she's in this dream, this golden moment can last forever, or at least for a lifetime.

CHAPTER TWENTY-TWO

Dawn admires the bright purple-blue flax rolling past outside the car window. It's interrupted every now and then by a field of shockingly yellow canola. She takes in the vibrant colours and tells herself to let any moment of beauty be enough. She's working on it—working on not losing herself completely to the despair that laps constantly at the edges of her perception. Working on making sure she keeps seeing the beautiful things. The trick is to remember they're both always there.

The drive back from Martin's new place calms her, especially now that it's summer. The house is in a minuscule town a thirty-minute drive west and is borderline ramshackle, on the edge but not part of a new development of identical beige stucco homes. It's a fixer-upper, undoubtedly, but fixing it up has kept Martin busy when he's not on the road, and Dawn has been coming over to help sporadically.

They have not heard from Cody since the night he vanished, which makes it a little over six months. Six long months of Dawn biting her tongue, holding back what she knows happened to her brother (*but what really did happen?*).

She told her dad that Cody left with Tyler to work in oil, or construction, or mining—she can't remember which, but they got hired by the same company and couldn't turn down the pay. She was vague and strained for casual but didn't achieve it, stumbling on the clumsy lie, but Martin seemed satisfied with it.

When Dawn returned from the clearing she laid in bed for three days. The house felt like a thing spent, and a few weeks later, out of the blue, Martin announced he was thinking about selling it and moving out of town. Dawn didn't pause before saying, "Yeah, I think you should."

The house took a while to sell, so Dawn kept herself busy applying for jobs and searching for apartments she'd be able to afford with the money Martin promised her from the sale. It wouldn't be a fortune, but it would be enough to get her started, get her set up.

Finally, the house sold and a downtown youth centre called her back and offered her a role helping to plan activities for the evening drop-in program. They were desperate enough not to ask for the references that weren't listed on her resumé and this made her feel simultaneously bad for them and glad for herself. She found an apartment she could afford and Martin co-signed for it, which, along with the money, compelled her to feel unbridled gratitude toward her father for the first time in years.

The pay at her new job is not good and she works just under the number of hours that would qualify her as a full-time employee, but it's a community-run organization and Dawn is drawn to a gritty gentleness in most of the staff, a distinct caring that's present during regular, everyday meetings and when visitors to the drop-in are disruptive or break the rules.

The majority of the youth that use the drop-in are Native—mostly Anishinaabe, Cree, and Métis, their families from the city or from one of the reserves and settlements that dot the surrounding prairies. Dawn stays and listens to the workshop sessions whenever she can, learning from her co-workers to make and present tobacco ties to Elders and knowledge keepers, her hands clumsily folding the fabric around the offering, moist from her palm. Their words and teachings settle inside Dawn, expand inside her, whisper to her that a sore heart can beat a different way. On Tuesdays and Thursdays, a tall man with a greying beard and a wonderfully low, resonant voice teaches beginner Anishinaabe lessons. Dawn isn't able to learn much, can't focus on something this intricate right now, but she does learn how to say rabbit: waabooz.

At odd moments now Dawn will feel the tug of a half-there memory, from somewhere deep in the shrouded depths of those fucked-up months. Snatches of Martin announcing he was going on vacation. Of Cody sitting tensely across from her at the food court, telling her to leave. Of the clearing. Almost all her memories from that time are fragmented and blurry, like she's trying to recall them through a thick fog. Whole chunks of time are completely gone. She suspects it must be similar for Martin. Sometimes when they're working on his place together she notices him staring off into the middle distance, frowning.

She still wakes most nights with her thoughts racing and tangled, images flashing like neon signs: Cody and Tyler marching toward her, Jake throwing Crystal into the void. Although she'll never hear the language that opened the portal again in her waking life, she hears it repeatedly in her dreams. She breathes in the night air and tells herself, *It's over*, even though she knows it's not.

For Sale signs went up overnight at both the Cleary and the Reed houses, followed by the arrival of moving vans a week later. Once Dawn feels steadier on her feet, she'll start her search for answers with Mrs. Cleary.

If her brother is alive somewhere, Dawn will find him. She still loves Cody, but she feels a hundred other feelings, too, all crowding each other, all taking turns shouting for her attention. She feels awful, on the whole, but some-times she doesn't. And she's learning to lean into those times when she forgets to be wracked with guilt or shame or anger, to let herself feel joy, or silliness, or just relaxed.

She doesn't like to remember her brother's vacant eyes.

Her heart fights against the knowledge of Cody's rage, his impulsiveness, his easy charm that got him nowhere in the end. The sidelong looks from white women all his teenage years and his stricken face when their mother died. Some void grew in the centre of him, a bloodline void shared by Dawn. She knew intimately the feeling of that interior chasm, like always being slightly out of place no matter where she was, like a constant, steady pull of unattributable grief at the base of her rib cage.

She wonders if causing someone else pain gave him some release from the presence of that void. Gave him something else to feel, something like power. But only a terrible, temporary power.

There was no trial.

Cody took a plea deal on the advice of his jaded public defender and was sentenced to ten years for manslaughter. Cody said that Jeremy had the knife, that Jeremy pulled it on him, but he managed to wrestle it away. That Jeremy kept coming at him. Self-defence. *But how? How could Jeremy have drawn the knife, pinned against the side of that garage?* As far as Dawn knows, nobody questioned Cody's story, and the police didn't bother to investigate, so the many needed answers were never found.

The lawyer and the judge were dispassionate to the point of not caring, and no one from Jeremy's family showed up to the brief court session. Jeremy's mom and step-dad had moved to Saskatchewan with their other kids a few months after it happened, both to get away and to be closer to family. They couldn't afford the time off work from new jobs to attend the sentencing, and they wanted to put what happened behind them anyway. It turned out Jeremy had grown up in a series of foster homes, scattered like land mines across the prairies, until his mother regained custody when he was ten years old.

Dawn only learned this after Jeremy was dead. Shortly after Cody was sentenced, she gathered what she could from the obituary and the single article in the local paper, from a few half-hearted Google searches that turned up scant details. Then she stopped looking for any more information about him. She decided she wasn't going to learn anything that would change anything, so there was no point. But really, she just couldn't bear to know.

The central, irrefutable fact of that night is that Cody killed Jeremy, and he will always have killed Jeremy, and Jeremy will always be gone. And the more real Jeremy becomes, the more crushing the weight of this fact.

As she nears the turnoff, she turns the radio down, feeling that blaring pop music is somehow disrespectful. She drives slowly down the dirt road, clouds of dust kicking up around her car in the dry August heat. The sky is impossibly blue, full of huge fluffy white clouds like a painting. This immense sky encompasses all that lies beneath it— great beauty and great pain.

She hopes she can find what she's looking for before she has to go. She has plans with Maureen, a new co-worker. They're meeting at Al's for a quick happy-hour drink before dinner reservations at a new fusion place downtown that Maureen's been wanting to try. Maureen is funny and weird and has a laugh so loud you can hear it from down the hall. She speaks to the youth with a frank kindness that Dawn admires intensely, though it also makes her feel nervous to imagine her own self being able to be so open. When Maureen first heard Violet's last name, she said, "Hey, so we're cousins!" She playfully hit Dawn on the arm with the back of her hand, and Dawn looked away to hide her smile.

Dawn parks in the small lot, cuts the engine, and closes her eyes. She searches for that hum, that buzz she can feel somewhere deep inside her ever since that night in the clearing. She finds it. Like electricity licking faintly over her skin. She hasn't seen her mother's ghost since that night, but she knows the hum is Violet. Somehow, she knows.

She opens her eyes and grabs the bouquet of plastic flowers off the passenger seat. She's never visited a cemetery before; they'd scattered Violet's ashes in the river like she'd asked for. Dawn feels unsure and awkward making her way along the rows, consulting the map on her phone, unsure how to read it. In short order, she is lost. She feels ridiculous. She feels ashamed. Like this is a cosmic sign that she should not have come, that she should not have had the gall to come. The wind chatters through the poplar leaves, and she hears within it an admonition. She should just turn back, *go*.

And then, by accident, she's standing over top of Jeremy's grave. It's a simple bronze plaque in the grass, engraved with his name, the date of his birth, and the date of his death. She kneels on the ground in front of the plaque because it feels right to be touching the earth and brushes stray bits of grass off its surface. She touches her fingertips to the metal. Dawn feels keenly the finality this metal plaque represents, the life that ended on that engraved date. She places the bright plastic flowers on the plaque and puts a rock on their stems so that they won't blow away.

ACKNOWLEDGEMENTS

This book was written in Toronto and Winnipeg and I am grateful to both places, and the people in them, for different things, and in different ways.

Thank you to my publisher, House of Anansi, and thank you and deepest gratitude to my editor, Shirarose Wilensky, for believing in the initial draft and for helping to shape this into the story that I wanted to tell; gratitude and thanks also to assistant editor Leslie Joy Ahenda.

Thank you to Jason Ryle for reading an earlier version and, always, for your feedback, advice, and insights.

And thank you from the deepest place within me to Mom, Dad, Maggie, Dag, Elowyn and James, for your love and support.

ADRIANA CHARTRAND is a mixed-race Native woman, born and raised in Winnipeg, Manitoba. Her father is Red River Métis (Michif), born and raised in the Métis community of St. Laurent, and her mother is a mixed white settler from Manitoba. Adriana has two degrees in film studies and has previously worked in the social work field. She lives in Toronto and works in the film industry.